NANCY WARREN

Ultimate Concealer

A TONI DIAMOND MYSTERY

ISBN: ebook 978-1-928145-01-1

ISBN: print 978-1-928145-00-4

Cover Design by Stunning Book Covers

Ambleside Publishing

INTRODUCTION

Toni Diamond never believed she'd see her no-good ex-husband Dwayne Diamond again, not after he abandoned her and their baby sixteen years ago. But now she's a successful independent beauty consultant for Lady Bianca cosmetics, Dwayne suddenly wants back in her life -- or at least in her bank account. He convinces their daughter, Tiffany, to go to Vegas and visit the father she's never known. When Toni follows her runaway daughter, little does she know she's about to run smack into a murder. Dwayne Diamond is the chief suspect and it's up to Toni to prove Tiffany's dad didn't commit murder, by finding out who did.

This is the second instalment in the best selling Toni Diamond series, which began with Frosted Shadow, though the books can be read in any order. Sexy detective Luke Marciano is back, and of course Toni couldn't go to Vegas without her mother, the Dolly Parton-obsessed Linda Plotnik along for the ride. While Toni noses around Vegas she and her mother find plenty of scope for their talents as sales-woman and makeup artists in this humorous Las Vegas set mystery.

ULTIMATE CONCEALER

CHAPTER 1

There are no ugly women, only lazy ones.

— HELENA RUBINSTEIN

"If I put on enough makeup, I feel like I'm someone else," Donna Ray Atkins said. "But then, when you work on a pig farm, you usually want to look like someone else."

Donna Ray's smiling face came through on Toni Diamond's computer screen along with the faces of the other five members of her top tier sales team. As Independent Beauty Consultants for the Lady Bianca line of cosmetics, each of these women were as important to Toni's business success as she was to theirs.

She loved the video conferencing technology that allowed her to talk to her team each week from the comforts of their own homes. She used this time to pump up the team, to strategize ways to boost sales, and to hang out with women she liked.

"I feel like I am showing the best me I can be," Suzanne Mireille said, the slight French lilt in her voice adding drama to her words.

Toni wrote the comments down in her notebook, thinking she might make up some slogan cards for her girls.

"I put my Lady Bianca makeup on in the morning, then I look at my face in the mirror and I see success!" Ruth Collier chimed in. A retired school teacher, Ruth was making more money in her second career than she had in her first.

"I love that," Toni said. "You are so right." She sat in the home office of the house she'd bought herself thanks to her success selling cosmetics for Lady Bianca. "And speaking of success," she said as she leaned forward, closer to the screen. "The monthly sales report is in." She pumped her fist in the air. "We beat our sales targets for the month, sold a higher volume than last month. Once again, we are the top sales team in Texas."

Toni didn't think of herself as a ruthless woman, but rather that success floated all boats. And the better other sales teams performed, the more inspired she and her sales associates became, spurred on to offer a few more free facials and makeovers to their friends, family, colleagues, and women in the grocery store. However, she wasn't above a little fist pumping in the privacy of her own office and with her own team.

She also wasn't above using the fresh information as inspiration to her girls, the sales recruits she'd brought into the business. She loved every one of them, and she loved their success. Of course, each tube of lipstick and each pot of face cream they sold not only netted them a commission, but also brought Toni a tiny scoop of the gravy as their sales director. A lot of small commissions could certainly add up.

When she finished the conference, she sent an immediate email blast to every sales rep in her region. "Hey, girls! We are slicker than this season's Berry Parfait Lip Gloss. Our team is number one again this month. Congrats to all of you for your hard work. I love you! Toni."

"I love you? You have got to be kidding," a bored and cynical teenage voice drawled behind her right shoulder.

Toni's perfectly manicured hand flapped to her chest, a flash of sparkle from the diamond rings on her fingers sparkling in her peripheral vision. "Oh, my goodness, Tiff, you startled me." She turned to glance at her sixteen-year-old daughter, filled as always with a combination of love and exasperation at so much youth and beauty hidden under the scowl and black, shapeless clothing.

"Sorry, just needed to check that my gag reflex was still working."

"I do love them," she said. "Some of those women were struggling single moms like I used to be. I helped them find a way to look better, help other women, and make money. I am proud of every one of them."

"Yeah, yeah. I've heard it all before."

Tiffany slouched to the big pink corkboard where Toni hung inspirational quotations, lists of ideas, and her weekly, monthly and yearly sales targets. In the center of the board was an article she'd cut out of *Texas Today* magazine. The article was a profile of successful Texas business women. Toni was interviewed about direct selling techniques. Tiffany took one of Toni's fake diamond-headed push pins in her black-manicured fingers and attached her own notice to the board.

"What's that, honey?"

"An article I found on the Greenpeace website about how the chemicals in makeup are poisoning the earth."

"You know, every month where sales are as good as this one means more money in your college fund."

"Not going to college, Mom."

Since Toni strongly suspected that this statement, like the Greenpeace article, was an attempt to irritate her, she bit her tongue and counted to ten. Then eleven. Twelve. At thirteen, she felt calm enough to open her mouth without screaming, "Of course you're going to college. You're too smart and too talented not to." Tiffany could claim she wasn't going to college, but her grade point average argued otherwise.

Instead she said, "Well, if you don't go to college, I can use the money to redecorate your room. I'll turn it into a boudoir where I'll throw home parties and recruit new Lady Bianca reps. Yep, we'll destroy the earth, one Fiesta Mocha eye shadow at a time."

"Oh, Mother."

Toni swiveled away from the computer. "Why don't you and I go shopping? We haven't gone for ages. We could check out the new summer fashions. Maybe get your hair cut?"

"Can't. I'm meeting Tish and Jenn. We're doing a project for the enviro club. Can I borrow the car?"

"The car?" Toni opened her eyes so wide her mascara-coated lashes poked her upper eyelids. "What about global warming?"

Her daughter's voice dripped disdain. "We're, like, carpooling."

Toni knew her daughter had been well-trained behind the wheel. She'd paid for the driver's ed courses. But it was still difficult for her to hand over the sparkly key chain without a pang. "Drive carefully, okay? Don't let those girls talk you into anything foolish."

"Nah. We won't get wasted until after the meeting." Then she cracked the grin that always melted Toni's heart and left.

Toni brewed herself a cup of coffee in the single-brew machine she'd won for hitting the top sales mark in her region last quarter. She knew herbal tea was better for her health and her skin, but she'd accepted long ago that she was never going to be perfect. She was doing the best she could.

She carried the hot, steaming brew up to her office and resettled herself at her desk. She took another moment to stare lovingly at the excellent sales numbers. When she checked her email, she wasn't at all surprised to find that most of her team had responded to her message with enthusiastic congratulations and excitement. Of course, the fact that they'd all answered their emails so fast suggested that they were also working on a sunny Saturday, one of the reasons why her team did so well.

Knowing that if she spent too long gloating over last month's results she'd waste this month, she closed the window and began strategizing on ways to market the newest line of lip glosses. It seemed to Toni that these would interest young mothers. "Little League," she mumbled as she made some notes for herself. "Must infiltrate Little League."

Her phone rang.

Before picking up, Toni swiped fresh lipstick over her mouth, inhaled positive energy and smiled. Whoever was on the other end of her phone could without doubt use a makeover, would like to host a home party, or, even better, wanted to sell Lady Bianca cosmetics.

"Hello," she said in her most welcoming tone. "Toni Diamond speaking."

"And don't you sound as pretty as a summer's day," a deep, sexy male voice replied.

Her smile fell off her face and dread clenched her stomach. "Who is this?"

"Oh, honey, don't you know?"

She did, of course, but she willed the caller to be a telephone marketer, a politician fishing for votes, an obscene caller. Anyone but—

"Your own husband?" His voice was still warm and sexy. A woman could lose herself in Dwayne Diamond's voice—and many a woman had—only to find herself abandoned when something newer and shinier came along.

"You haven't been my husband for sixteen years, Dwayne." He'd left her shortly after their daughter was born. Besides their daughter, the only thing he'd left her with was his fancy last name.

In a second, she was plunged back to those early months after he'd left. She'd had no money, no skills. Barely more than a child herself, she'd had to figure out how to raise a baby on her own, keep some kind of roof over their heads and pay for food. She'd done it, too. Stubborn pride and a desperate need to keep her baby safe and healthy had driven her. Her mother had helped out where she could, but Toni had refused to become that sad cliché, the teenaged single mom living in her own mother's basement. Besides, her mom didn't have a basement. She lived in a trailer.

When a well-dressed woman had offered the young Toni a makeover while she picked over bruised apples in a discount supermarket, she couldn't have known then that she was Toni's fairy godmother, but so it had turned out.

Toni had embraced Lady Bianca and home sales with an energy that came partly from need and partly from discovering that she was a natural-born saleswoman. She loved people, she loved makeup and she really, really loved watching her income increase from a few dollars that first month to more than a hundred the second month.

She was on her way.

"Doesn't mean I don't still care about you."

And no two-bit charmer was going to hurt her now. "What do you want, Dwayne?"

"I wanted to congratulate you, honey. I got this here glossy magazine in front of me, and it says you're a real successful businesswoman." Her smile might have dropped to the floor but his was plastered all over his face. She could hear it oozing over the phone line, as fake as his protestations of love had been.

"Thank you. Now I've got to g—"

"Whoa! Not so fast there, honey. We've got some catching up to do. When I saw that picture of you in the magazine, and saw you were as pretty as ever, I figured it was time we got reacquainted."

"I don't think so."

"Toni, you used to be a lot softer."

"I wonder what toughened me up."

"Listen, let me buy you a drink. A cup of coffee."

"You're in town?" Horror sharpened her tone. He'd left Dallas as well as her and moved to Austin, which she'd only discovered when a very pissed-off woman had called a few months later looking for him.

"I could be on the next plane."

"Plane?" It was a three-hour drive, give or take, to Austin.

"Sure, babe. I'm a headliner in Vegas." The only place she could imagine Dwayne being a headliner was at a lice convention. He was a country singer with a good voice and songwriting skills that were derivative at best. She suspected most of his success was due to looks and charm which he had far too much of.

"No. Thank you. I don't want to have a drink with you."

"Darlin', it would be worth your while. I've got a business proposition for you, you being such a top businesswoman and all."

She refused to scowl. She wasn't getting wrinkles for Dwayne D. "Dwayne, did you seriously call me up after abandoning me sixteen years ago to ask for money?"

"I'm not asking for a gift, sweet pea. It's an investment."

"An investment. In what? A new guitar?"

"I don't just play country and western music." He sounded stung. "I'm diversified."

"I bet you are."

"Look, if you're not interested in an investment, I'll take a loan."

She didn't know whether she wanted to laugh or cry. "Dwayne, please don't ever call me again."

"Don't hang up." She heard a tone that hadn't been there before. He'd dropped the smarmy tone and something sharp came through. "We haven't talked about that sweet daughter of ours. How is she?"

Toni practically had to pry her teeth apart to get words out. "She's fine."

"You tell her hi and that I'm going to come and see her

real soon. We've got lots of years to catch up on." In the background, a woman called his name, and he said, "I've got to go now, but I look forward to seeing you both real soon."

When she got off the phone, she found that the fingernails of her left hand had dented half-moons into her palms and one of the diamantes she had embedded into her nail tips had come out, leaving a small round hole in her nail like somebody had shot a bullet through it.

CHAPTER 2

I don't have a girlfriend, but I know a woman who'd be mad at me for saying that.

— MITCH HEDBERG

*R*age. She recognized the emotion even though she hadn't experienced it for a long time. Rage. Directed at Dwayne D. Diamond.

Toni couldn't settle to work. She couldn't settle to anything. In fact, she couldn't stand her own company cooped up in her house. She'd go to the salon, that's what she'd do. Take comfort in the familiar ritual of a manicure. Even if it was a week ahead of schedule, she would not go an entire week when a hole existed where a diamond ought to be.

But when she got to her garage and the space where her pale mauve Prius usually sat was empty, she remembered she didn't have a car. Tiffany had it.

She grabbed her cell phone out of her bag, speed-dialed Linda Plotnik.

"Mom," she wailed when Linda answered. "I need you. Can you come get me?"

And the wonderful thing about a mother, whether her daughter was sixteen or thirty-four, was that, of course, she did.

Toni was waiting outside on the curb when the mauve Cadillac screeched to a halt—with "Here You Come Again" blasting out the windows. Her mother's obsession with Dolly Parton, which used to embarrass Toni into a coma, now seemed endearing. She only hoped Tiffany would grow similarly appreciative of her own eccentricities given enough time.

When she jumped into the passenger seat, her mother said, "Baby, what's wrong?" before Toni even had time to buckle her seat belt.

"Dwayne called."

Her mother's generous cleavage almost catapulted out of her apricot tank top when she gasped. "Dwayne Diamond?"

"Yep."

As they drove to the salon, Toni filled her mother in on the call.

"He abandons you and your infant daughter. Doesn't see either of you for sixteen years." She turned left, so wide she nearly took out a Humvee, which honked loudly as it swerved. "And not one single cent does he ever send you. And he's got the nerve to ask for money?" She was so angry her platinum curls were smacking her cheeks as she ranted.

"Pretty much what I thought," Toni said.

There was silence but for the sound of Dolly. Then Linda asked, "Do you think he'll try to get to you through Tiff?"

And that, of course, was the part that Toni didn't even want to contemplate. "I think he said that to piss me off. He's never wanted to see her before, why would he now?"

"Does she still ask about him?"

Toni shook her head. "Not for a few years now."

"We should have told her he was dead like I wanted to."

"But he's not dead."

"And ain't that a surprise? I thought for sure some jealous husband would have put a bullet through his cheatin' heart by now."

"Yeah."

"I'm sorry, honey. Some girls just don't have any luck."

Somehow, the salon and her mom helped Toni get back on track. Dwayne was a no-good, cheating loser. Irresponsible and childish, he used his charm and good looks to drift through life, rarely challenged by anything approaching morals. But she didn't think he'd contact Tiffany. An almost grown daughter would make him feel old, she suspected.

She'd said no to giving Dwayne money and that was most likely the last she'd see or hear of Dwayne for another sixteen years. Or sixteen million, if she was lucky.

Her diamond restored to the tip of her nail where it belonged, sparkling with the other nine, and a pedicure thrown in for the heck of it, helped her the way therapy might help another woman. To Toni, being surrounded by women laughing, gossiping and relaxing, with her mother for company, was as good as a group counseling session.

When she got home, even Tiffany was in a better mood.

"How was enviro club?"

"Really cool. And I'm sorry about your car. The man said it would be good as new with a new bumper and engine and a couple of new doors."

"You are so grounded forever."

Tiffany laughed. "I put the keys beside the fruit bowl. What's for dinner, Tiger Mommy?"

"Oh, I don't know." She opened the fridge. "How about mushroom lasagna and salad?"

"Or we could have pizza?"

"Pizza and salad. Honestly, for a vegetarian, you don't eat enough vegetables."

They chatted over dinner and Toni thought, as she had so many times over the past sixteen years, that Dwayne had missed out on the only good thing he'd ever done.

She managed not to think about her deadbeat ex for the next few days until she was startled by her daughter coming into her office one evening after dinner.

She fiddled with one of the silver rings on her hand.

"Mom?"

"Mmm-hmm?"

"Why did you and Dad break up?"

Toni's head jerked up from the Spring Fling sample packs she was packing into her tote bag to take to a Spring Fling makeup party. Toni didn't do a lot of home parties anymore but she liked to keep her hand in.

"What brings this on, Tiff? You haven't asked about your dad for a while."

Tiffany hadn't inquired about her father for probably two years. How creepy that she would ask about him today, only a few days after Toni had received a call from Deadbeat Dwayne.

"I don't know." Today Tiffany had chosen to embrace spring and its colorful palette by wearing more black than usual. "Most of my friends who have divorced parents still see their dads. I feel like a freak."

Toni couldn't stop herself from smoothing a loving hand down her daughter's back. "We were way too young to get married. I wasn't much older than you are now. And Dwayne, well, he certainly wasn't ready to settle down. He lit out when you were a baby and I haven't seen him since."

"But he's older now. Maybe he wants to see me. Maybe he feels like you're keeping me from him."

"Has he contacted you?" The words were out before she could contain them. Her tone sounded sharp even to her own ears.

"See? There you go acting all control freaky. What if he has? Doesn't a man have a right to see his own child?"

Feeling as though a giant fist were squeezing her heart, she said, "Of course he does. I'm surprised he'd want to get in touch after all these years, that's all."

"I'm old enough to know the truth," Tiffany said, looking achingly young and lost in a way Toni knew she could never fix.

"I've always told you the truth."

"Have you?" And before she could answer, Tiffany's cell made a tone that indicated a text was coming in and she was gone.

Toni did not believe her daughter's sudden interest in her father was a coincidence. She also understood that Tiffany was a lot like she herself had been at sixteen. Stubborn, convinced she knew about life. Naive as hell.

If only she knew how to protect her daughter from her own father.

～

LUKE MARCIANO WAS knee-deep in a murder investigation. Not that you needed to be much of a detective to solve this case. Two neighbors had exchanged angry words and insults over the placement of a fence. A fence, for chrissake. Half the neighborhood had witnessed the altercation. Then, a day later one of the two was found in his backyard with a couple of bullets in him. The other neighbor had a cabinet full of guns and one was missing. Luke sometimes felt like everyone in his adopted state solved their problems with guns.

When his cell rang and he glanced at the incoming number, he wondered whether his day was about to get better, or worse. With Toni, you never knew.

"Marciano," he said.

"Honey, you know it's me. Why do you always bark out your name? You think I might have forgotten it?" She had the sexiest voice. He sometimes wondered if that's why she was such a successful saleswoman. But he doubted it. More likely it was because she was so pushy.

"Force of habit," he said.

"Am I interrupting anything?"

"Murder investigation."

She sighed. "Don't people in this state ever do anything but kill each other?"

Her words so mirrored his own thoughts that he had to smile. "Texans like to do everything bigger." He glanced around, making sure no one could hear him. "Speaking of which, you still coming over to my place later?"

He and Toni had an interesting relationship. Having met on a murder investigation where her smarts—well hidden, in Luke's opinion, under more makeup and diamonds than any woman needed—had almost got her killed. Since then they'd become, he wasn't really sure what. Friends with benefits maybe came closest.

Between their two insane work schedules and her teenage daughter, they didn't see a lot of each other. When they did, they got together at his place for an evening. They'd order take-out or one of them would cook. With the divorce rate in his profession so high—and he'd already struck out once—he knew how difficult it was to sustain a relationship. He suspected Toni was equally skittish of anything resembling permanence.

"I sure am. And good news. Tiffany's sleeping over at a friend's. I can stay the night."

He felt his day getting better by the second. "That is very good news."

"I'll see you later."

When she arrived at his place later, he kissed her, and he could tell right away something was up. "What is it?"

She lifted a hand to her chest and the reflection of five tiny diamonds winked at him. "Tiffany's going through something."

"Tiffany's always going through something," he reminded her.

"I know, but this is different. It's about her dad."

"What about her dad?"

"I think he contacted her. He called me out of the blue

trying to get some money out of me, if you can believe it. He saw that article in *Texas Today*. He doesn't even live in Texas. Somebody must have sent him a copy."

Toni never talked about her ex, but from the few hints she'd dropped, the man did not sound impressive. "The guy who ran out on you and left you with a baby is hitting you up for a loan?"

She nodded, her curls glinting in the light. "I think he might have contacted Tiffany, as well."

He knew how much she protected her daughter. Too much, in his opinion, but he didn't have kids, so he kept his feelings to himself. "She's sixteen. What harm can he do her?"

"She's my baby, Luke. I don't want to see her hurt."

He pulled her closer, if that was possible. "What makes you think he contacted her?"

"Because she asked about him. Said a father has a right to see his daughter, which sounded exactly like something Dwayne would say, when he's tried very hard for the past sixteen years not to see her, or know about her and definitely not to support her. I couldn't even find him for the divorce. Had to do that without him, too."

"Probably it was coincidence," he said, kissing her. Not that he believed his own words, but he didn't have much to offer.

The next morning, Luke was barely in the office when Toni called. He picked up with a grin. "Hey, sexy."

"I want to report a missing person," she said, sounding unlike herself. No smile in the voice.

"What happened?" But in his gut, he knew.

"It's Tiffany. She's gone."

17

"You know where she's gone, right?"

"Yes. She emailed me this morning."

"The sleepover?" He was pretty sure there hadn't been any sleepover, which gave Tiffany a big head start.

"There was no sleepover." She tried to stifle a sob, which sounded more heartrending than an actual sob.

He scanned through everything he knew about teenaged runaways. "Her cell phone must have GPS. We can track her."

"She left her cell in her room. The messages were all wiped clean." She sighed. "I'm looking up the phone log online; at least I'll be able to see what numbers she was calling and texting, but none of the content."

"Hang tight. I'm coming over." There wasn't much he could do, but Toni needed him.

As he headed out, he said to Henderson, his partner, "I'll be back in a couple of hours."

"But we brought the guy who shot his neighbor in for questioning. I was going to put him in the interview room."

"Put him in the holding tank. Let him sweat."

TONI COULDN'T PANIC. She knew emotion could only make her do something foolish. Still, when Luke arrived she wanted to throw herself against his strong chest and sob. But Toni didn't have time for weakness. She had to find her daughter.

He pulled her to him and hugged her anyway, as though knowing how much she needed it. "Tiffany's smart," he said against her hair. "She'll be okay."

"But how's she getting to Vegas? What if she's hitchhiking?"

"Let me see the email she sent you."

"Of course. I'm sorry. I can't seem to think straight." For the first time since she had joined Lady Bianca, Toni had no cosmetics on. She hadn't even combed her hair or dressed. Her robe swished before her as she ran upstairs to her office. The article Tiff had pinned to her corkboard fluttered as she opened the door, filling her with a pain so sharp she almost couldn't breathe.

The email was still open on her computer screen. All she had to do was push a button on her keyboard to get rid of her screensaver, the kaleidoscope of relentlessly positive motivational mantras that seemed pretty hollow right now.

Success wasn't achieved in a series of small steps. Right now, success would be achieved when she got her daughter home where she belonged.

Luke sat in her office chair and she read the message over his shoulder, as though it wasn't burned into her brain.

"Hey, Mom," it began. "Don't worry. I'm going to visit my dad. He and I both figure it's time we got to know each other. I know you don't want me to go, but I have a right to know my own father. I'm fine. My schoolwork's up to date. I'll call you when I get to Vegas. DON'T WORRY! Love, Tiffany."

Apart from the nagging drag of fear, she felt furious with both of them. "That's Dwayne, right there. That line, I have a right to know my own father. That's him. Putting ideas in her head."

Luke turned his head and regarded her, his dark eyes serious. "She does have a right to know her father," he said.

"He abandoned her. Plus, she's underage. Can't the police do something?"

He shook his head slowly. "She's getting close to the age of emancipation. With no sign of foul play, and an email telling you where she's going, which is to her father..." He made a gesture with open hands that seemed very Italian considering he'd been born in the States, and clearly implied that the cops weren't going to rush out and bring her daughter back home.

"Her father," she exploded. "He can come here and see her if he wants a relationship so bad. Why the hell would he want her to go to Vegas? It's not like Dwayne. He'd never want to be bothered with a teenager. She'll remind him he's getting older. She'll be an expense. She'll sure as hell curtail his sex life."

"Think about it, Toni," he said in his calm way. "If you're right about Dwayne, and I really hope you're not, he wants Tiffany there for one reason. To get to you. He wants money."

"That low-life snake. Oh, that's sleazy even for him. He'd kidnap his own daughter to get money out of me?"

"Toni, it's not kidnapping. He is committing no crime whatsoever."

"How can you say that? He abandoned her, never sent a dime—"

"He also never signed any divorce documents, right?"

"No. Because I couldn't find him and I couldn't afford to track him down. I got divorced without him just like I did everything else without him."

"So he's not violating the terms of a custody agreement because he never signed one. His daughter decided on her own to go see him. He'll act delighted to see her, and he's got to know that you'll be there almost as soon as she is. He wants money. You want your daughter back. Maybe he's looking at this as a simple business proposition."

"He's not that smart," she snapped.

Then she put her hands over her face and pressed her palms into her burning eyes. She gave herself a minute, then said, "You know, I am so tempted not to go. Let her spend a few days with Deadbeat Dwayne. She'll appreciate how good she has it with me."

"That's an excellent idea."

If it was somebody else's kid, she'd think so too. "But what if she's hitchhiking? Anything could happen to her. She's only sixteen."

"She's not hitchhiking." He grabbed her shoulders and squeezed. "Come on, Toni. She's your daughter."

"Dwayne never came to get her. And she doesn't have the money to fly."

"My guess is she took the bus."

"The bus?" She could barely stand to think of her baby riding a long distance all alone on the bus.

"Did you check her phone records?" She knew he dealt with murders and terrible crimes all day long and was thankful he was taking her missing daughter seriously.

"I printed them out. Lots of calls to the same number Dwayne called me from." She picked up the printout and handed it to him. "I've sheltered her. I know I have. I over-compensate because I'm a single parent. My mom thinks I feel guilty because I chose such a loser to father my child."

"Your mom is a lot smarter than she looks."

"I should have listened to her when I was young. She told me Dwayne was no good for me."

Everything about this mess was stressing her out. While she watched, he scanned the numbers rapidly. Then he banged a blunt fingertip onto a number. "That's the number to buy bus tickets. That number right there."

It wasn't a huge relief to find her daughter had taken a bus hundreds of miles, but it was better than hitchhiking.

"Did you call Dwayne?"

"Of course I did. Got his voicemail."

"You leave a message?" He sounded wary.

"Honey, please, I'm also a lot smarter than I look. I did not say anything except, 'Please call me.' There's nothing he could play for Tiffany that would make me sound like a hysterical witch."

"Good." He kissed her. "Tell me what you need."

She looked at him knowing he meant what he said. "Dwayne's not listed in any directory I can find. All I have is his cell number and he's not picking up."

He nodded. "I've got a buddy in LVPD. I'll get you everything I can on him."

"Thank you. I can't get a flight out today. Everything's booked. I'll head out tomorrow morning."

"Okay. I'll get back to you as soon as I can."

"Luke?"

"Yeah?"

"Can you do one more thing for me?"

"What?"

She hated feeling needy, but she felt like her head was going to explode from worry. "Could you stay with me tonight?"

He nodded once. "Yeah."

CHAPTER 3

I cannot think of any need in childhood as strong as the need for a father's protection.

— SIGMUND FREUD

iffany Diamond scraped a ribbon of black nail polish off one thumbnail with the nail of her opposite thumb. The bus rolled along with boring monotony. A fat woman with BO sat beside her, melting over from her seat into Tiffany's. She pushed her earbuds deeper into her ears as though she could drown out her own thoughts. But they wouldn't be drowned.

What if he didn't like her? What if he was disappointed? She hadn't sent a picture. Hadn't thought of it. He'd sent her one, though.

Her dad looked kind of like Bradley Cooper. He had the same killer smile and the confidence of someone who'd always been hot. She scraped off another ribbon of black. The silver skull ring on her index finger gleamed. He'd known her mom back when she was the same age as Tiffany was now.

She'd seen photos of her mom when she was young and she'd been all blond hair, cuteness and boobs. If he thought they looked alike, he was going to be sorry. She wished she'd got her hair cut. She wanted to think about something else, but it was tough with Dwayne singing in her ear. He'd sent her a couple of tracks off his latest album. The country and western songs made her think of Dolly Parton, which made her think of her gran.

The bus dragged on past small towns and fast-food joints. She slept a little and ate a granola bar she'd packed from home and sipped on a bottle of water, but she didn't have much of an appetite. She felt like she was coming down with the flu or something. Kind of dizzy, nauseated from the endless movement of the bus and the smell of the woman beside her.

The lady beside her got off the bus in Kansas City, which made her feel less squished, but more alone. People had probably guessed the woman was her mom.

Most of the people on the bus seemed excited to be going to Vegas. Like they were going to come back millionaires or something. A group of loud guys in their twenties joked about driving back home in a limo. Yeah, right.

They were passing around a bottle. One of them tried to pass it to her, but his buddy said something to him. All she heard was jail bait. And after that, they left her alone.

When the bus finally pulled into the station in Vegas, she was exhausted, a little car-sick—bus sick, she supposed—and her stomach was so clenched she was having trouble breathing.

She was almost glad the fat man in front of her was taking his time packing up his stuff. It gave Tiffany a few extra minutes to pull herself together.

She was hyperventilating when she walked through the grimy doors into the bus station.

Stop it, she mentally yelled at herself. Of course he'd like her. She was his daughter, wasn't she?

He'd found her on Facebook, that's how he'd finally got in contact. She'd immediately messaged him her phone number and he'd called her right away. It was like a Disney movie in real life. When he'd called she'd almost cried. He sounded so happy to talk to her. Dwayne had told her on the phone that he'd wanted to see her for a long time but her mom had stopped him. She wouldn't even give him Tiffany's cell phone number.

Tiffany had always suspected her mother was partly to blame for her having no dad, not even a weekend and summer vacation dad. Other kids might complain about having stuff at two houses and drama between the exes, but at least they knew their own fathers.

It had seemed like such a good idea to avoid the inevitable fight with her mom. Get on the bus and tell her mom after. Easier to ask forgiveness than permission, Dwayne had said with a chuckle. Now she kind of wished she'd waited.

It was just nerves, she reminded herself. She glanced swiftly around the waiting area almost sick with excitement, but unless he'd changed gender, race or gained a hundred or so pounds, Dwayne Diamond wasn't among the handful of people obviously waiting for her bus.

She gave him ten minutes and then wished that at least

she had her cell phone with her. She'd seen on TV how easy it was to trace people with cell phones and her mom was dating a cop. But it would have been comforting to have her phone with her.

Could he have forgotten? Got sick? Been in an accident?

Worse, had her mother somehow found out and used her cop connections to have Tiffany's father thrown in jail or something?

Wild thoughts chased around in her head as she fidgeted on a hard bench until finally she noticed a payphone stuck to the wall. She'd never used a payphone before. She had to read the directions twice and then she fumbled and dropped the money before getting the hang of the thing. She'd written down her father's cell number, but she didn't need to look. She'd memorized it.

"Darlin'," he said, picking up right away. "I'm on my way. Hold tight, I'll be right there."

Twenty minutes later, the door opened and her father walked in. He wore a white Western-style shirt, jeans that were pretty tight and cowboy boots. His smile was so big she felt warmed by it. She rose, thinking it was going to be okay.

When he saw her, he slapped a hand over his heart and took a step back. "Can this be my baby girl?" he yelled.

She nodded, stupidly shy.

He looked so happy to see her she felt her shyness melt. Especially when he held out his arms wide. "Well, come on over and give your daddy a hug!"

This is my father, she thought, as she found herself squeezed into a hug. He felt warm and solid. He smelled like cologne. She thought it might be the one called Stetson.

He grabbed her bag and threw it over his shoulder. When

they walked out of the bus station, Tiffany noticed the bored-looking woman at the ticket counter checking her dad out. She felt a flicker of pride that he was so hot.

There were a few cars parked outside, but when she saw the vehicle he was headed toward she cried out involuntarily. "Omigod, is that yours?" It was a cherry red, long ride that was so retro she felt like she needed big sunglasses and a silk headscarf tied under her chin to sit in it.

He chuckled. "Sure is. My pride and joy. This here's a 1965 Corvette. You know anything about cars?"

"No," she said, running her hand over a red fin.

"You drive?" he asked her.

"I just got my license," she said, not without pride.

"All right then. Tomorrow, when you've got your bearings a little, you can drive."

She smiled at him gratefully. She thought she'd probably be too nervous to drive his pride and joy, but it was nice he'd asked. They cruised down a busy street with the top down. She had an impression of noise and color and more glitz than one of her mother's makeup conventions, but mostly all her attention was on the man beside her. The man she'd been dreaming about and weaving stories about since she was old enough to dream.

"Now tell me everything I've missed in the last sixteen years," he shouted over the wind.

She held her long hair back in a fist to stop it whipping in her face. She wasn't sure what to tell him. Her life seemed like a lot of not much, and she really doubted he wanted to know about when she got her first tooth or walked or what childhood diseases she'd suffered. Finally, she said, "I'm pretty good in school. I'm on the honor roll."

He grinned over at her. His teeth were so white she suspected he had them professionally whitened. "Smart girl, huh? Good for you. You popular?"

Not even to impress her father would she lie. "No. Not really. I have a few friends, but..." She shrugged.

"You got a boyfriend?"

She snorted. "The boys in my school are complete losers." She didn't want him to think she was pathetic, though, or totally awkward around boys, even though she was. So she added, "I've had a couple of boyfriends, but there isn't anyone now."

"A pretty girl like you is only single by choice."

She liked that notion, so she nodded as though it were true.

"You ever been to Vegas before?"

"No," she said, reminded once again that he knew nothing about her, this man who was responsible for half of her genetic material.

"You are going to love it. It's like a party all day and all night, every day. I work hard, don't get me wrong, but I play hard too. I've got a lot of friends I want to introduce you to. Places I want you to see."

He drove as though he didn't have a destination and didn't care. As though all he wanted to do in the world was cruise around talking to her. She thought about how crazy busy her mom always was and then felt a pang of guilt. She knew her mom would be pissed. Also worried. She'd have to email her the first chance she got.

"Is there an Internet café around here?"

He sent her a sharp look. "Honey, you're on holiday. What do you need the Internet for?"

She hesitated. "I should email Mom and let her know I'm okay."

He drove on for almost a block then said, "Why don't you leave your mom to me. She's already called and left a message." He shot her a sideways glance. "I'm going to tell you right now, your mom ripped me a new one." He shook his head. "I haven't been called some of those names since, well, I guess since she threw me out back when you were a baby."

Tiffany stared at him. She felt as though her world had tipped a little from its usual orbit. "Mom always told me you left us."

He pulled over, wheeled the big car to the curb and stopped so he could turn to look at her, such sincerity in his eyes that she couldn't look away. "How can you think that I would ever leave you?" He shook his head. "Now, your mom is a wonderful woman and I will not say one word against her. I admire what she's done, I truly do. But, you know what they say. There are two sides to every story. I'm not saying your mother was wrong to throw me to the curb, and I'm not saying she was right. But I deserve a chance to get to know the child I never knew."

"But...I... She should have told me the truth."

"I agree. But let's not worry about that now. You hungry? I bet you are. I know a great place where the burgers are the best you'll get outside our home state." He pulled back into traffic while Tiffany's mind reeled.

His cell phone rang a lot, she noted. Obviously, a '65 Corvette didn't come equipped with Bluetooth, so he checked call display and either ignored the calls or took them while driving. A big no-no in driver's ed.

Only one call caused him to pull over and stop the car.

"Dwayne Diamond," he said in a fake cheerful voice that reminded her of the Lady Bianca ladies practicing cold calls. He glanced over at her and whispered, "I gotta take this. I'll be a second." Then he pushed open the car door and walked a ways down the sidewalk. He walked in front of a peep show, then a pawn shop and finally a discount liquor place, then he turned and paced back again. She couldn't hear what he was saying, but she got the sense that he was getting some bad news.

She tried to interest herself in her surroundings, but she was getting a sense of unease deep in her stomach, the way she felt facing an exam she hadn't studied enough for. He'd left the car engine running and his CD was playing, the same one she'd listened to coming in on the bus. As one track ended and there was a pause before the next began, she heard him snap, "Yeah, I'm on it. You'll have your money. You've got my word on that, sir."

She wanted to ask him if everything was all right, but the second he was back in the car he started telling her about all the people he wanted her to meet. "My friends, they're as excited as I am to have you back in my life."

"Me, too," she said.

He pulled the big car into a gravel lot outside a roadhouse called Buck's Steakhouse. "Wait until you try the burgers. They do one with blue cheese and bacon that will knock your socks off."

She climbed out of the car and followed him inside. The place was half-full. A woman with platinum ringlets and freckles stood near the front. When she saw Dwayne, her face lit up. "Darlin' Dwayne," she cried and threw her arms around him giving him a big, smacking kiss right on the mouth.

"Marlene, I gotta introduce you to my daughter. This here's Tiffany."

Her round eyes grew rounder. "You got a kid?"

"Sure do."

"Pleased to meet you," she said, looking at Tiffany as though she couldn't imagine how Dwayne had fathered someone so much less gorgeous than he was himself. "Right this way."

She led them to a table near the bar. Dwayne said "Hi" or "Howdy" to half a dozen people before they were seated. The woman brought menus, but he motioned them away. "Two of the choicest burgers you got, the ones with the blue cheese and bacon."

"Fries or salad?"

"Actually," Tiffany said, "could I just have the salad?"

Dwayne stared at her. "You're not some kind of vegetarian, are you?" he asked in the same tone he'd use if she were an extraterrestrial, a zombie, or a communist.

"'Fraid so."

He shook his head. "I never would have thought any daughter of mine would become a vegetarian."

"I can do you a dinner salad, no meat," the server said.

"That would be great."

"Well, I'll have the burger. And bring us a couple of beers."

The woman glanced at Tiffany, who was five years away from twenty-one, and said, "Sure thing."

"What did you think of Marlene?" her dad asked when the woman left.

31

"Is she your girlfriend?"

"Hell, no."

"Good, because she looks like a Raggedy Ann doll." She wished she'd bitten her lip. Why did she always blurt out those stupid things? It was like she thought them, and out they slipped.

But instead of being offended, her father threw back his head and laughed. "She does. That's exactly what she looks like. Ha-ha."

She sipped her beer slowly and ate her salad while her dad wolfed down his burger, tearing into it with strong, white teeth. He offered her a fry. "Or are you a frytarian too?" he teased.

She laughed and helped herself to his fries, dipping them into a blood-red pool of ketchup.

He finished his beer and ordered a second. "You want another?"

She shook her head. She liked beer, but she didn't want to get wasted on her first meeting with her father.

When they were done, Marlene appeared with the bill. "Put that on my tab, will you, honey?" he said. He pulled out a five and dropped it on the table. "And this is for you."

"Oh, Dwayne," she said, sounding less than thrilled, and she took the bill folder away with her, leaving the cash on the table.

"Okay, sweet pea. Let's go," he said, rising and pulling on his denim jacket.

"Dwayne!" a man called. "Hold up."

Her father turned, held out his hand, looking delighted. "Holman! Good to see you."

Holman grabbed the hand briefly. He held the bill folder in his hand. "Look, Dwayne, we can't—"

"I want you to meet my daughter, Tiffany. She's visiting her old dad for a few days. Isn't she gorgeous?"

The guy named Holman stared at her with hard, black eyes. "You really his kid?"

"Yes."

She felt a weird vibe between the two men and she didn't like it. After a moment, when the guy named Holman fidgeted and mumbled under his breath, he finally said, "You're right, Dwayne. She's a beauty. Call me tomorrow."

"Sure will, old buddy."

"This town is all about who you know," Dwayne told her as he started the car. "You see, I send a lot of business Holman's way. He hasn't let me pick up a dinner tab in months. That's how it works in Vegas."

"Oh." Hadn't looked that way to her.

"Now, I perform at a little club in a casino. I'd be honored if you'd come and watch your old man perform. Be a real thrill for me."

"Yes. Of course. Sure."

"The old homestead's not much," he warned, "but I've got all my capital tied up in a business venture. When the deal closes, the first thing I'm going to do is buy you your own convertible."

"That's okay. You don't have to."

"I'm your father. I want to. A smart girl like you, who works so hard at school, should have a reward."

"Thanks."

"Thanks, what?"

"Thanks, Dad."

"That's better. You keep on calling me Dad. We've got a lot of time to catch up on."

He turned and gave her his heart-melting grin.

Tiffany had never been to Vegas before. Well, truth was, she'd never been much of anywhere. A couple of lame school trips, a road trip to Florida with her mom, and a truly humiliating pilgrimage to Dollywood in Tennessee for her grandmother's birthday one year, that was about it. So, she was excited to see what all the fuss was about. Most of the musicians who'd played Vegas were legendary. Elvis, Sammy Davis Jr., and even Celine Dion. She knew her father wasn't a legend, obviously, but she was ready to see him perform. Even try to get past her distaste for country music.

She hadn't loved the tracks he'd sent her, but she suspected her dad was the kind of performer who was meant to sing live.

Slowly, he backed the Corvette out of its parking space and began to move forward. Then something hit the car with a crunching sound of metal on metal and she was thrown back against her seat. Her father's smile turned to an expression of shock and rage. "What the hell?"

A black Cadillac had hit them. As Dwayne jumped out of the driver's side door and strode over to the other vehicle, a red-faced guy got out. Dwayne stopped when he saw the guy. "What the hell, Grant? You could have killed me. And my daughter."

Grant didn't seem too concerned. "You got something of mine and I want it back. Next time I won't play around."

"I don't know what that crazy wife of yours has been saying, but you know I would never—"

Two really big guys got out of the car, front and driver's

side. She didn't like the look of them. They were like extras out of a thug movie. She grabbed her bag, scrabbling for her cell phone to call 9-1-1. In a panic her fingers grasped and searched, scraping over ancient pieces of gum and loose change, before she remembered she'd left her cell phone back at home.

"Help," she screamed, already pushing open the car door, thinking to run into the restaurant. Even as she moved, the door to the restaurant opened and Marlene came out, followed by the owner.

In the slow motion horror of a dream, she saw that scene from a bad thug movie get played out in front of her. The two guys stalked forward.

"Come on, guys," Dwayne said. Then, "Grant!" before Thug One grabbed his arms and Thug Two slugged him in the gut.

As he doubled over and his legs buckled, he cried out, "Not the face. Please. I gotta perform tonight."

CHAPTER 4

Women's natural role is to be a pillar of the family.

— GRACE KELLY

*L*uke showed up at Toni's that night with a pizza and a bottle of red wine. There were times in a woman's life, Toni mused, when a man with a pizza box under his arm was a very welcome sight. Especially when the man was Luke Marciano.

He'd obviously stopped off at home to change, and when he pulled her in for a kiss, she could tell he'd showered. His hair was still a little damp and she could smell his shower gel.

"How are you holding up?" he asked.

"I'm okay. As much as I would like to slowly strangle Dwayne right now with one of his prized bolo ties, he is her father. He's not going to let anything happen to her."

Luke's mouth twisted in a hastily suppressed grin. "Seriously? Bolo ties?"

She patted his shoulder. "Don't worry, I have better taste in men now."

"Obviously."

He followed her into her the kitchen and while she served pizza on her pretty pale green plates, he opened and poured the wine.

They settled on the couch in the den. Not even the cloud of testosterone hanging around Luke like a swarm of mosquitos could tone down the femininity of the room but he didn't seem to mind.

While they ate, he filled her in on Dwayne's whereabouts. "You couldn't find him because he's got no address."

"He can't be homeless." Even Dwayne wouldn't invite his own daughter to go live with him under a bridge.

"No. The house is registered to a numbered company."

"Not his?" Unless the number was zero.

He shook his head. "It's a CPA who owns the house. Brent Hodgkin. I'm guessing your ex rents a room. But it's in a respectable part of town," he said, answering the question he must have known she'd ask first.

She nodded, knowing she wouldn't be happy until she'd seen Tiff for herself and urged her to share a hotel room with her for a few days while she got to know her dad. If Tiff had made up her mind she was going to spend some time with her father, well, she was going to do it. Toni had spent some time thinking today and decided the best thing she could do was to stay in Las Vegas herself until Dwayne inevitably lost interest in chaperoning a teenaged daughter around and broke her young heart.

"What's your plan?" Luke asked.

"I'm going to play it by ear. So long as I know she's safe,

I'll try not to be too hard on her." She pressed her lips together for a moment, then let them go. "I think I'll stay in a hotel for a few days with plenty of room so she can stay with me if things aren't as rosy as Dwayne's pictured them."

"What do you think the chances of that are?" Luke asked, his dark eyes regarding her.

"Oh, I'd guess about one hundred percent."

"Poor kid."

"Yeah."

He pulled a computer print-out from his pocket. "This is the address where Dwayne lives. I've also added the contact info for my buddy. If you need anything, or Dwayne pulls any kind of crap you don't like, well, my friend's the kind of guy who can let a man like Dwayne Diamond know that messing with you, or your daughter, is a bad idea. All off the record, of course."

She smiled. "Thank you for this."

He nodded briskly but didn't meet her gaze. She watched him for a second. He might have a truly excellent cop face, but she knew this man pretty well. "What aren't you telling me?"

"It's nothing. Dwayne's not unknown to the cops down there, that's all."

Her stomach did a swan dive. "Define not unknown."

"He made free and easy with a woman's credit card to the tune of a few grand. She was going to press charges and then next thing you know, claimed it was all a mistake. A lovers' quarrel."

"He always did make fools of women."

"She'll be okay," he said again, knowing she was thinking of Tiff.

"Yeah. She will."

"You need a ride to the airport?"

She shook her head. "My mom's driving me. But thanks."

"Then I guess there's not much more I can do." He leaned forward, his dark eyes teasing and mesmerizing. "Unless I can help you take your mind off your troubles."

She nodded, and he took her hand and led her to the bedroom where, for a few hours, if he didn't make her forget that her only daughter had run away from home to visit her deadbeat dad, at least her cares were pushed to the back of her mind for a while.

In the morning, Luke headed out early, kissing her on his way out. "Call me if you need anything."

She watched him head out the door. "Hey," she called as he opened it.

He turned.

"Thanks," she said.

Since Toni had spent the afternoon the day before canceling all her appointments and reshuffling her responsibilities to other members of her team, she had nothing to do this morning but pack. The task didn't take long since she was scrupulously organized, and she'd packed plenty of times for conventions and business trips. She estimated she'd be in Las Vegas for four days and packed clothes for six just in case. Her traveling makeup bag was always packed with this season's colors and because she never, ever, left the house without promotional items, she packed the smaller of her sample bags. By nine she was fully made-up, her hair done, and she was ready to go. She'd dressed casually in a pair of jeans with a pattern of rhinestones on the butt, her leather boots, a blue shirt and a light jacket. She hesitated over her jewelry. Normally, she liked to display the gorgeous rings she'd won over the years for sales performance. The bling not only reminded her every time it flashed before her eyes that she was meant to sell Lady Bianca, but the jewelry also reminded every woman who sold Lady Bianca cosmetics, or who might one day sign up to sell them, that there was money to be made.

However, her personal financial success was not something she wanted to broadcast to her lowlife ex.

It cost her a pang to lock up the best of her jewelry, but she still had enough sparkle about her that she could live with herself.

When her mother pulled up in front of the house, she said, "I've got wonderful news."

Since Tiffany wasn't sitting in the passenger seat of her mother's boat of a car, she couldn't imagine the news could be all that wonderful. "You've heard from Tiffany?"

Her mother's bright expression faded. "No. I haven't. But the good news is I don't want you facing Dwayne Deadbeat Diamond by yourself." She beamed. "I am coming with you."

"But, are you sure—"

"Yes. I've booked the flight. They had space. We're going to get our baby back."

Toni couldn't imagine her mother was going to be a huge help. On the other hand, she didn't have a lot of time to waste trying to convince her to stay put. "One rule, Mother."

"What rule?"

"You are not allowed to shoot Dwayne."

Her mother put her well-powdered nose in the air. "I'm not even bringing a gun."

"Good."

And they set off.

When they arrived at McCarran Airport, the first thing Toni did was turn on her phone. The first thing her mother did was to head to the slot machines with a squeal of delight.

There were three missed calls on her cell phone from Dwayne's number. Three voice messages. As she was attempting to retrieve the messages, the phone rang again. Dwayne. She answered immediately, an unpleasant constriction squeezing her chest. "Dwayne? Where is she? Tell me she's okay."

"Mom?" Tiffany sounded panicked.

"Tiff, what's wrong?"

"I'm not sure. But I think Dad might be in trouble."

If Dwayne wasn't in some kind of trouble that would be news, but Toni didn't say that. Instead, she said, "Where are you?"

"I'm at Dad's house. Mom, I know I screwed up and shouldn't have left without telling you, but could you please do something for me?"

"What is it, honey?" Though, in her heart, she knew what was coming because she knew Dwayne and she knew her daughter.

"Could you come to Vegas and help Dad?"

"Already on it," she said.

She collected her mother from the slot machines and they went to fetch the rental car she'd booked. They could take taxis but where Dwayne was concerned, she wanted to know she could always get away.

With her mother navigating using her cell phone app, they soon found the house. "You're sure this is it?"

"It's the address you gave me."

The house was a surprise. Clean and modern, with a big garage out front and enough windows upstairs that there must be at least three bedrooms, it looked like something a suburban family would live in. It was close to downtown and she imagined the rent must be reasonable for Dwayne to live here.

She parked in the driveway in front of the closed garage door and they approached the front door. "You let me do the talking, Mom. Okay?"

"Uh-huh."

She rang the bell and in no time at all, her daughter opened the door.

"Mom!" she cried and threw herself into Toni's arms the way she'd done when she was much younger.

"Oh, Tiff," she said, hugging back fiercely. "I'm so glad you're all right."

"You gave us quite a scare, honey."

"Gran!" And then Tiff was hugging her grandmother. "Come on in."

She was going to ask where Dwayne was when she stepped into the house and glanced around. Her senses were immediately overloaded. All she could say was, "Oh, my."

Tiffany giggled. "I know. It's like you walk into the world's most boring looking house and step into the Arabian Nights or something."

A tart's boudoir was the term on Toni's tongue but she kept her mouth shut. The wall colors were vibrant jewel tones and when Tiffany led them into the living room off the front hall, she almost expected to see Mae West reclining on the red velvet chaise that held pride of place in the room, asking some young man to peel her a grape.

The walls were purple with gold molding framing the ceilings, and the armchairs and sofas were upholstered in rich damask. The walls were covered with movie scenes and advertising from the '20s and '30s. A rich white shag rug covered the floor, but as though a big area of white were too dull, huge red and gold silk cushions offered extra seating.

"I think my eyeballs need a nap," Linda said, after glancing around.

"And your father lives here?" Toni asked.

"He says it's temporary. But the owner's really nice. You'll like him."

"Where is your father?" Toni asked, refusing to be side-tracked.

Tiffany put a fingernail to her mouth, a habit she'd broken a couple of years earlier. Toni noticed that her black nail polish was nearly all scraped off. She took her hand away from her mouth before she got to chewing her nails. "He had to get his car fixed," she said.

"You didn't call me in a panic because your dad's car needed a tune-up. What's going on?"

"I don't know, but I think he's in trouble."

"Now there's a shocker," Linda said, seating herself on the divan. With her platinum ringlets and cleavage-baring red shirt, the black trousers and gold heels, she fit right in.

"Sit down and tell me about it," Toni said, drawing her daughter to the couch.

"These guys crashed into Dad's car yesterday afternoon." She wrapped her arms around herself and leaned forward, almost unconsciously assuming the crash position on an airplane. "Then two of them came over and punched him."

"Hmm. Now the jealous husbands are buddying up."

"Mother!"

"Sorry." And Linda made a lip-zipping motion.

"Were you there?"

A miserable nod.

"Oh, honey, were you hurt? Do you have whiplash? Have you seen a doctor?"

"No. It wasn't a big crash, it was more like they wanted to scare him."

"With his daughter in the car?" Toni wanted to scare her ex-husband a little herself. With her bare hands.

"They didn't know I was his daughter. Obviously. Anyway, when he got back in the car, he was pretty shaken, but he said it was a misunderstanding, and then he had to perform last night." Tiffany glanced up at her mother's face and then down at the glass and gold coffee table as though riveted by the copy of *Glamour* that lay atop it. Toni noticed that the *Texas Today* magazine that had caused Dwayne to call her out of the blue was tucked beneath *Glamour*.

"Did he take you with him?" She could imagine Dwayne wanting to show off for his daughter, but the thought of him letting a sixteen-year-old girl sit in the audience unattended was enough to get her chewing her own nails. Fake diamonds and all.

"No. He wanted to, but Brent, he's the guy who owns the house, he said you have to be twenty-one."

And thank you, Brent, Toni thought to herself.

"I sat home last night and watched TV, but then this morning I heard Dad talking on the phone. He said...." She swallowed before continuing, "He said, um, he said he thought his life was in danger. And I thought, since you solved those murders at the Lady Bianca convention, that maybe you could help save Dad."

Linda made a strange sound, as though she were shouting without opening her zipped lips.

"Then I will need you to be a lot more specific. Who was he talking to? What were his exact words?" Tiffany had an excellent memory, and she'd inherited Toni's powers of observation.

"Don't get mad. Remember, you two haven't been married for a long time."

"So, he was talking to a woman?"

Tiff nodded. "He said, 'Aw, now come on, honey. You know I'm good for it. Our ship's going to come in, and I'm going to take you to Paris and treat you like a princess.'" Tiff had always been a good mimic, and as she repeated Dwayne's words, she'd even fallen into his way of drawling his words. That she was getting a word-for-word account of the conversation, Toni had no doubt.

"Then he paused for a bit, like the other person was talking, and then he said, 'Because somebody's trying to kill me, that's why.' And then I think he hung up. I didn't hear any more."

Tiffany and Linda exchanged a quick glance. Toni tried to come up with a diplomatic way to tell Tiffany that her father was not only a liar, but a huge drama queen. Finally, she said, "You know, Tiff, sometimes people get carried away and say things for effect that they don't really believe. Why would anyone want to kill your father?"

"Mom, you didn't see those guys who crashed into his car. It was like out of a gangster movie. There were two big guys, like the muscle, and then the third guy who was obviously in charge. Dad knew him. He called him Grant."

"You think this Grant is trying to kill your dad? Seems pretty stupid to rough him up and threaten him in front of a witness. He'd be the obvious suspect if anything happened to your father."

Tiffany pushed her long hair behind her ears. "The guy, Grant, he said, 'You got something of mine and I want it back. Next time I won't play around.' Then Dad said, "I don't know what your crazy wife's been saying,' and then they hit him."

"I wouldn't call that a death threat," Linda said. "He never said anything about killing your dad."

"Dad says he lent Mom money to get her business started back when I was a baby and she promised to pay it back. He says he needs that money back now."

"Oh, I am gonna kill that lyin', cheatin' sonofagun!" Linda shouted, jumping right up out of the chaise.

"Now that's a death threat," Toni said.

CHAPTER 5

You must do the thing you think you cannot do.

— ELEANOR ROOSEVELT

Toni explained to Tiffany that her father had never lent her money for her business. She stopped short of telling her daughter that he'd sneaked out in the middle of the night. He'd left her and her baby girl without a backward glance.

Looking back, Toni knew now that he'd done her the biggest favor of her life. From the heartbreak and shock of discovering that her young husband was a no-good, cheating snake who had no intention of providing for his only child, she'd learned to survive. And then she'd learned to thrive.

But at the time, she'd believed her world had ended.

The afternoon was getting on and Linda had declared her intention of taking the three of them out to dinner somewhere nice when the front door opened.

Expecting to see Dwayne, whom she had not set eyes on since he'd left them, Toni felt her muscles contract. But the man who walked through the door wasn't Dwayne. He was a tall, slim man, with short, wavy brown hair, glasses, and the nondescript clothing of a civil servant. He wore a plain gray suit, with a white shirt and a blue striped tie. He carried a simple black briefcase.

"Hi, Brent," Tiff said. "This is my mom, Toni. And my grandmother, Linda."

This had to be Brent Hodgkin, the CPA who owned the house, but surely this dull-looking man wasn't responsible for the decorating. She wondered if he'd bought the house from a color-blind silent movie fan and never got around to redecorating.

"Toni," he said, walking forward with his hand outstretched. "It's a pleasure to meet you. You have a really nice daughter." His voice was rich and resonant, and when she shook his hand she noticed that his skin was soft.

"Thank you. It's nice of you to let her stay."

"No problem. I've got lots of room."

He shook Linda's hand next. And Linda, who never met a single man she didn't think might be marriage material for her daughter, said, "I'm taking the girls to dinner. Why don't you join us?"

He put his briefcase down and pushed his glasses more firmly onto his nose. "That's nice of you, but I'm afraid I have to work tonight."

"Oh, that's too bad." She glanced at his briefcase. It was pretty obvious that he was newly arrived home from work. As though feeling some explanation was necessary, he said, "I have a second job."

"It's a tough economy, all right," Linda said. "And I understand Las Vegas was hit real hard."

"Yes," he said faintly. Then, "Well, if you'll excuse me," and he picked up his briefcase and left the room.

"Honey, we're going to go check into the hotel now. Why don't you come with us? We'll get a suite and use the spa. It will be a girls' vacation. You can see your father whenever you want."

She could see that Tiffany was torn. Finally, she shook her head. "I think I should be here when Dad gets back."

Linda started to speak but Toni kicked her ankle and spoke over her. "Okay, Tiff. We'll pick you up for dinner at six."

"Why didn't you make her come with us?" Linda wanted to know as they pulled away from the curb.

"Because she needs to find out what her father is like, and we need to let her. Maybe they'll figure out a way to have some kind of relationship. I don't know."

"I know you're right but it makes me crazy that Dwayne is feeding her that line of bull."

"I know."

They headed to the hotel, Toni feeling a lot better now that she'd seen Tiffany, and checked in. The room contained two queen-size beds, a small seating area with a pull out couch, a chair and a built-in unit with the TV. The bathroom didn't have nearly enough counter space for two women who not only made their livings selling cosmetics, but who also believed wholeheartedly in their benefits.

While they were prettying themselves up for dinner, Toni checked her messages. There was one from Patience Vernon, one of her newer recruits to the Lady Bianca team. She returned the call while Linda re-did her face.

Her smile was so automatic that she didn't even notice she was beaming with positive energy when she pushed send on her cell phone.

"Patience! I was so happy to get your message. It's Toni Diamond." She always identified herself even though all her team had call display. She'd learned in one of the many sales seminars she'd attended that it was a good practice both to assume anyone calling you was offering good news and always to give your name. With anyone other than her own sales team, she'd usually identify herself as Toni Diamond of Lady Bianca Cosmetics since she knew every time she linked the two together a little more cosmetics karma went out into the world.

"Hi, Toni," Patience said when she answered. Toni did not receive beams of positive energy coming back her way.

She pulled up Patience's file on her computer. They'd worked on sales goals together and, since Patience was a beginner, they were starting with friendly fishing. Her goals were small enough to be readily achievable which would lead to a feeling of success, and that would spur her on to larger goals and greater success.

Toni always found, however, that getting that first flush of success was critical.

"I bet you're calling to tell me that you've already booked your first makeover. Maybe even got someone in your circle interested in selling Lady Bianca at a home party." Patience was a member of a church with a large congregation. She also worked for a multi-national company. She had all kinds of opportunities to go friendly fishing in her own pond.

"I'm not sure I'm ready. There are so many people, so many other Lady Bianca reps offering makeovers, I'll only make a fool out of myself."

Toni didn't let her smile dim, not by a single watt. She reminded herself that her newbies were like toddlers. They had to be encouraged to walk, and the next thing you knew they'd be running all over the place. "Okay. The first thing we need to work on is attitude."

She gave a pep talk and at the end of it, Patience had agreed that she would go to her women's circle at the church tomorrow night and talk to at least three ladies about her exciting new venture. In fact, she'd committed to talking to as many as ten ladies, stopping only when she'd booked one for a makeover.

When she put down the phone, her mom was putting the final swish of Raspberry Parfait gloss on her plump lips and staring at the result critically.

"Was that girl calling you to quit?" she asked, as she turned from the mirror.

"Oh, sure. The newbies usually get cold feet at least once. I've got her reenergized. All she needs is one success and she'll start to feel that fire in the belly."

They passed the time during the short drive back to Brent Hodgkin's house arguing whether a makeover or booking a home party was the most exciting success for a new recruit.

When they got to the boring house with the exotic interior, they walked up the path, her mother insisting she wanted to take a photo of the living room on her smartphone as she wanted to do something similar with balloon curtains in her home. Since Linda's double-wide was already a shrine to her idol, Dolly, Toni wasn't sure the curtains were going to match but she kept her mouth shut. She rang the doorbell and waited.

She pictured Tiffany with her blow dryer going, unable to hear her. She pulled Tiff's cell phone from her bag so she'd remember to return it and they could communicate again.

When the door finally opened, a stunning woman stood there. Tall, slender, with cascades of blond ringlets and floor-length showgirl costume, she said, "Come in. Tiffany's almost ready."

In the second blink, Toni recognized that under the makeup, the wig and the glam, was Brent Hodgkin, the dull-looking man who owned the house.

Her mother must have made the connection about the same time for she said, "Oh, you're a tran—" She turned to Toni. "What do they call those?"

"A female impersonator," Brent said in that rich, low voice that was so much more at home in this persona than in his daytime one.

"What's your act called?" Toni asked before her mother could speak another word.

"Sunny and the Three Chers," he said. "I'm Sunny. With a u."

"Oh, I get it," Linda said. "Where are the three Chers?"

"We'll meet at the club later."

Toni asked, "Do you and Dwayne work together?"

"Yes. That's how we met. We're part of the floor show at the Double Nugget Casino."

"The Double Nugget?" Linda asked. "Is that on the strip?"

"It's one of the older casinos," Brent said. "It had its heyday back in the '50s when the Rat Pack dominated Vegas."

Toni didn't know much about Vegas but she knew that the

old downtown had very much gone to seed, giving way to the new strip with the big, glitzy places like the Bellagio and the Venetian where shows tended more to Cirque du Soleil than Sunny and the Three Chers.

The Double Nugget was to the strip as Dwayne Diamond was to Neil Diamond.

"So singing is your second job?" Linda asked.

"Yes." He seemed so much more confident and interesting than he had earlier.

"I've always wanted to sing." She pushed out her already more than ample chest and said, "A lot of people say I look like Dolly Parton."

"You do," Brent said politely.

Before her daughter arrived on the scene, Toni asked, "Do you know what kind of trouble Dwayne's in?"

Brent looked at her and said, "Dwayne courts trouble the way other men court women."

"And vice versa," Linda muttered.

Toni knew there was a lot he wasn't telling her, but she also suspected that now wasn't a great time to be asking. He was probably keyed up about performing. She remembered from when she'd been with Dwayne that he was always even more self-obsessed than usual when he had to perform that night.

So she nodded. "I'll see how Tiffany's doing."

"You missed a spot," Linda said.

"Pardon?" Both she and Brent/Sunny turned at once, but Linda was looking at Brent/Sunny's chest.

"You missed a spot when you were shaving your chest." She came a step closer. "And that's a nasty rash. What kind of moisturizer are you using?"

Toni held her breath, but Brent/Sunny seemed happy to talk sensitive skin. When she left the room, her mom was already digging in her bag for a sample of the Lady Bianca sensitive skin moisturizer. "And if I may say so, I think we could find you a better palette of eye shadows for your skin tones."

"Really?" Brent/Sunny said, waving a well-manicured hand toward his eyes. "Because I am not in love with this purple."

"No. It's all wrong for your coloring. We don't have time tonight, but tomorrow I can bring over my kit and we'll see what we can do."

"And you think you've got something that won't irritate my skin?"

"Lady Bianca says put the drama on the skin, but the skin itself should always be calm. Well, she says it better than that because she's English, but you get the idea."

TONI FOUND Tiffany's room by following the sound of a blow dryer, as she'd suspected. She knocked on the door and found her daughter had already managed to scatter her belongings all over the guest room. But Toni also noted that she'd made an effort with her appearance. She'd put on some makeup in a color other than black and removed the traces of funereal nail polish.

She wore her usual tight jeans but on top she wore a green shirt that brought out the color in her eyes. Toni might feel a stab of irritation that it was her no-account father who was responsible for the change, but she wasn't going to argue with the improvement.

She was also too smart to comment.

"Grandma's downstairs and I think she's trying to talk Brent into a makeover."

"Oh, my God," Tiffany said, jumping to her feet and grabbing her black Toms off the floor. "She's been here for like five minutes and she's already pimping makeup?"

"That's your grandmother. Never miss an opportunity," Toni said with pride.

Out of respect to Tiffany's vegetarianism, Toni and her mother skipped the steakhouse they both would have preferred and settled on a restaurant that gave a great view of the strip.

Considering how upset she'd been with her daughter, the meal was surprisingly fun. She suspected that Tiffany had not enjoyed taking this trip all on her own as much as she'd anticipated she would. And, while she was a long way from seeing Dwayne in a clear light, she must be wondering why a respectable man would get beaten up in broad daylight and then refuse to go to the cops.

Toni didn't want her to see Dwayne as the complete loser he was, but she did want her daughter to realize that he was not a good man to idolize. She knew she had to tread carefully.

So, when Tiffany announced, "I have a surprise, well, really it's Dad's surprise."

She kicked her mother under the table before she could engage her mouth and asked, "Oh? What is it?"

"Dad's got our names down so we can get into his show for free tonight. Isn't that great?"

Dwayne might not be the sharpest knife in the drawer, but he'd always been smart where manipulating women was concerned. Of course he wanted his daughter to see him perform. He wanted to charm her along with every other female in the audience. He might not be the greatest singer, but he was a hell of a performer.

He'd been showing off his whole life.

CHAPTER 6

Beauty and folly are old companions.

— BENJAMIN FRANKLIN

The Double Nugget may once have been popular with the Rat Pack, but now Toni suspected it was popular with actual rats. It was down at heel, a little sleazy, and the casino they had to walk through to get to the show lounge was full of people who looked as though they might be gambling with their Social Security checks.

Even the sound of the slot machines was more shrill than the ones in their hotel, a tiny bit desperate.

"Look up," Linda said, nodding her head in an upward direction.

Toni and Tiffany did. The ceiling looked as though it needed painting and some patching done. It was stained with grime and the lighting was industrial. "See all those round things? Those are security cameras. They're everywhere in Vegas. I saw it on a show about secrets of Las Vegas."

"Doesn't seem like much of anything is a secret if there are that many cameras," Tiffany said.

The casino was so massive that there were intersections with signs giving directions to a buffet, the restaurant, one of a number of bars, and the Double Nugget Show Lounge, their destination.

"Oh, look," Linda said, staring hungrily at the brightly lit machines. "There's a whole bunch of machines based on *Dukes of Hazzard*. Maybe I could just—"

Toni grabbed her mother's arm and pulled her back. "No. There's a casino in our hotel. You can go down later."

They turned back but Tiffany didn't move. She stood stock still in the middle of the aisle. When Toni turned to her, she saw that her daughter looked pale and rigid. "Honey, what is it?"

"That's the guy who crashed into Dad's car. And those are the two guys who hit him."

She followed Tiff's gaze and it was easy to see who she referred to. Even in the crowded casino you could tell that this was a guy with power. He was big. Large in every way from his height, which had to be around six-four, to his bulk. He wasn't fat, but he was very solid, like a wrestler who'd lost muscle to fat. He had a square head and a short neck. Short hair, a blue suit that looked handmade, and too much gold jewelry.

The two guys with him were paler versions of himself. Classic sidekicks.

The three were standing, watching the action at one of the craps tables. Toni watched a waitress in a ridiculously skimpy outfit deliver drinks to the players. As she walked past, the big guy said something to her and she giggled and walked on.

She was headed toward them and as she reached them, Toni said, "Excuse me, who was that man you were talking to?"

She glanced back. "You mean Grant Forstman?"

She had no idea who she meant but she nodded anyway.

"He's my boss. He owns the casino."

"Oh. Thanks." If he owned the casino, then he had to be Dwayne's boss too. Was Dwayne really dumb enough to sleep with the casino owner's wife?

"Can I get you a drink? So long as you play, the drinks are free."

Linda said, "Well, isn't that ni—"

"No, thank you," Toni interrupted. "We're heading in to see the show."

"Okay. Have fun." And the waitress walked on.

Toni led them in a wide half circle around Grant Forstman. She did not want him to recognize Tiffany, and she did not want her daughter anywhere near that man or his muscle. "Do you want to leave?" she asked her daughter as they moved out of range of the casino owner.

"No. I can't let Dad down. I promised we'd be there."

"And there's a trait that did not come from his side of the family," Linda muttered so only Toni could hear.

The show lounge was a dim cavern with round tables scattered on two levels. It wasn't full to bursting, but it wasn't empty either. The young woman at the front desk looked as though she didn't get enough to eat or enough sleep. Even her over-processed red hair looked exhausted. Tiffany shyly told the woman that Dwayne Diamond was her father and that he'd left tickets for them.

The woman's eyes showed their first spark of life. "Dwayne has a kid?" She stared at Tiffany for a moment then said, "Huh." But she checked a list and nodded. "Sure. You can go on in. Sit anywhere."

Toni let Tiffany choose their seats and she picked a table on the second tier but near the front.

THE THREE CHERS' outfits made the original Cher look tame by comparison. How did they keep those headdresses from falling off? And how did they manage to dance in those shoes? Their show might be camp but it was well done. All four of them, including Sunny, had great voices, and Toni found herself laughing and singing along.

And then the MC announced "Country singing sensation Dwayne Diamond." Toni hadn't set eyes on Dwayne in sixteen years. When that familiar, long-limbed man walked onto the stage carrying a guitar, his boots adding a little swagger to his step, she fell back in time for a moment. How hard she had fallen for that man back when she was too young and stupid to see that this diamond was a fake.

Oh, but he sparkled like the real thing.

As he settled himself in front of a microphone, pushed his Stetson back and gazed out at the audience, he said, "How y'all doin' tonight?" She felt a hum coming from her daughter. It wasn't anything you could hear, more an energy. And she was helpless to stop her daughter from being pulled in just as she would be helpless the first time Tiffany had her heart broken.

He strummed a little on his guitar and said, "I am honored to have three very special ladies in the audience tonight. They came all the way from Texas. Tiffany, Toni, and Linda, this one's for you. It's called "You Are the Only One for Me.""

He'd written that song years ago. He told her he wrote it for her, and it wasn't until later that she found out he'd been telling the same story to a lot of women. Since no names were mentioned, it was an easy lie to get away with.

Dwayne had a pretty good voice. He sounded familiar, like you might have heard him on the radio. And that was his problem. He wasn't unique. He sounded a bit like a lot of big country and western singers. His songwriting didn't stand out any more than his voice did. But, in an intimate venue, with a lot of women in the audience, Dwayne could make you believe he was so much more.

He was thirty-eight years old and in his prime. She wondered if he still cherished hopes of being discovered.

HE CAME out after the show was over and headed straight for their table. "And how are my three favorite Texas gals?" he asked, his handsome face creased in a smile. Not a shadow of a doubt seemed to exist that he'd be welcome.

"You were great, Dad," Tiffany said, accepting the hug he bestowed on her.

"Thanks, honey."

Then he turned to Linda. "Why, Linda, I do believe you are prettier than ever."

"So are you, Dwayne."

It was true, too. He'd been boyishly handsome back when Toni had married him. The sixteen years between then and now had added a few wrinkles around his eyes and filled him out. He was a seriously hot guy.

When he turned his attention to Toni, his grin spread even wider. "Oh, honey, will you look at you? I have missed you." A stranger hearing him would have thought that she was the one who had left him. He pulled her into a hug whether she wanted to go or not.

"Hello, Dwayne," she said.

"Can you believe this gorgeous girl of ours?" Slight emphasis on the *ours*, as though one implanted sperm made him father of the year. He pulled up a chair from a neighboring table and sat down. He waved his hand for one of the wait staff, even though they were clearly cleaning up. "Louise, honey, I want to buy a round of drinks for my family here."

"Thanks, Dwayne," she said. "But we've been traveling all day. We're pretty tired. Let's get together tomorrow."

For a second his lips thinned and she saw the petulant teenager she'd known too well. Then he was back to being Mr. Jovial. "Of course, honey. Sure. Tell you what, you and Linda come on by the house tomorrow for breakfast. I'll make you my famous pancakes." He grinned over at Tiffany. "My daughter can be my sous chef."

"All right." She knew there would be a reckoning, and she was going to have to set Dwayne D. Diamond straight on a few things. Like the fact that her daughter was not a bargaining chip. And that he was never going to get a cent out of Toni. Tomorrow morning would be good.

"Well then, girls, let me walk you to your car."

"Aren't you coming?" Tiffany asked, sounding disappointed.

"No, honey. I can't. I've got a business meeting tonight. I'll be home in an hour or so. Don't you worry. I'm sure your momma can drop you off." He put an arm around Tiffany. "We'll have a good talk in the morning, before your mom and grandma get there."

She nodded, so smitten with him she couldn't even see how selfish he was.

He walked out with them, keeping up most of the conversation. Linda was uncharacteristically silent, for which Toni was grateful. She knew that if her mom started talking to Dwayne, it wouldn't be small talk.

They got to her rental car and he said good night to Linda, and "See you in a little bit" to Tiffany. They climbed in the car and when she would have followed, he put a hand on her arm. "Look, Toni, I really need to talk to you. This business opportunity is a very time-limited thing."

"What's her name? This business opportunity you're meeting at," she glanced at her watch, "eleven at night."

"I'm meeting Grant Forstman. He's the owner of the casino and a very well-connected guy."

She didn't so much as raise an eyebrow. Of course, he had no idea she knew that Forstman was the man who'd bashed up his precious car and had him thumped only yesterday.

"What exactly is this business opportunity, Dwayne?"

He came closer, dropped his voice even though there was

nobody in earshot. "How'd you like to earn a one thousand percent return on your money? In only a few weeks?"

"Anything with that kind of a return is a scam or crooked. Which is it?"

He ran a finger up her arm and stepped even closer. She could smell the Stetson cologne he'd worn forever. See how attractive he was with the tiny crinkles around his eyes. "All I want is to make enough money to start over. I know I've made mistakes. I look at that girl of ours and it breaks my heart I don't know her better. You do this one thing for me and I'll be able to leave Vegas. I'm thinking maybe I'll come home. We should be a family again, Toni. A real family."

He was angling his head, moving his lips infinitesimally closer to hers, exactly like a scene from a movie. "Dwayne, are you seriously hitting on me?"

The angling for her mouth stopped. "I find you very attractive, and you are the mother of my child. I am not hitting on you. I'm telling you I want another chance."

She resettled her bag over her arm. "Kidnapping my daughter and trying to use her to extort money out of me is not the best way to woo me. Just FYI."

And then she turned from him and got into the rental car, banging the door behind her.

"THERE'S plenty of room at the hotel, Tiff. Why don't you come and stay with your grandmother and me? They've got the movie stations. We could watch a movie while Grandma gambles your inheritance away."

"I—I can't. I promised Dad I'd stay tonight."

She knew better than to push. Seeing Dwayne tonight had reminded her all too well how stubborn a girl could be at sixteen. "Okay. But you call if you change your mind or want to talk."

"I will. Thanks, Mom."

They dropped her off and Linda called out to her, "Tell Sunny and the Three Chers to call me. Your mother and I can give them all a makeover. I think we've got some products that could really add to their show."

"I will," she said in a tone that sounded more like, "I'd rather eat maggots."

Toni turned to Linda. "Mother," she said.

"Yes, honey?"

"Can I apologize right now for what I put you through when I was sixteen years old?"

She nodded. "Doesn't feel too good, does it?"

She shook her head. "Sometimes being a mother sucks."

Linda nudged her. "It's still the best job in the world, though."

"Yeah. I know."

"Do I have to go choke down Dwayne's pancakes tomorrow?"

"You can talk makeup with Brent and do makeovers. Hopefully Tiff can help you and Dwayne and I can come to an understanding. As in, he needs to understand that he is not getting one penny out of me, and I will not have my daughter used like a poker chip."

There was a short silence. "Okay. For that I can choke down pancakes."

But they never did get their pancakes.

Toni and Linda were getting ready to leave for breakfast

the next morning when Toni's cell phone rang. "It's Tiffany," she said, surprised. Tiff rarely called. She always texted.

"Probably telling us Dwayne needs us to pick up pancake mix."

"Shhh," she said, then answered. "Hi, Tiff."

"Mom, you've got to get right over here." Her daughter sounded hysterical.

Every nurturing, child-protecting gene in her body leapt to attention. She had her car keys in her hand even as she said, "What is it?"

"It's Dad. He's been arrested."

"Arrested? What for?"

"Murder."

CHAPTER 7

The only way I'd be caught without makeup is if my radio fell in the bathtub while I was taking a bath and electrocuted me and I was in between makeup at home. I hope my husband would slap a little lipstick on me before he took me to the morgue.

— DOLLY PARTON

"*I* can't leave yet, I haven't finished my face," Linda cried. She had one false eyelash glued to her lid and the other hanging from one finger.

"Tiff needs us. Dwayne got hauled away for murder."

"Oh, for Pete's sake," Linda said, and pushed the other eyelash on so rapidly it went on all crooked.

"You can finish your makeup in the car," Toni cried as she ran ahead to press the button to call the elevator.

"What is the second commandment of Lady Bianca's Ten Commandments?" Linda asked as she tottered along behind her daughter.

"Never apply cosmetics in a moving vehicle," she replied. "But Dwayne's gone and broken one of God's Ten Commandments, and I think that might trump Lady Bianca's."

"Oh, I feel like a caterpillar is crawling up my eyelid," Linda complained, trying to fix the faulty lash.

"Who could Dwayne have killed?"

"I always thought he'd end up killed by a jealous husband, to tell you the truth. I never thought he'd do the killing."

"No." Toni felt as though her world had tipped sideways. The elevator came and they stepped in it. The downward swoop did nothing to restore her sense of balance. "He's a cheat and a liar and he'd steal and swindle if he had the opportunity. But I can't see Dwayne as a killer."

"You haven't known him in a long time. People change."

"But right when he's got his daughter staying with him? Why wouldn't he wait until she was back home if he was going to kill someone?"

"I don't know. Maybe it was an accident." Then she shrieked. "Oh, darn it, I just poked myself in the eye. Ow. Oh, now my mascara's going to run."

Toni drove as fast as she dared to Brent Hodgkin's house and pulled into the drive. Whatever drama had taken place was over. The house looked as respectable and dull as always.

She and Linda ran to the door. She'd barely rung the bell when the front door opened and Tiffany tumbled into her mother's arms. She'd obviously been crying. "Mom. It was awful. They came, and they had guns, like on TV. And they took him away in a cop car." She sobbed. "My daddy's not a murderer!"

Toni hugged her daughter to her, feeling the young body shake with sobs. "I don't think he's a murderer either, honey," she soothed. After a while, when Tiffany was calmer, she asked the obvious question. "Who is he accused of killing?"

"That awful man. The one who crashed into our car."

Toni got a very bad feeling in her gut. "You mean the casino owner?"

"Yes. Grant Forstman."

The man Dwayne had said he had a meeting with late last night.

"Let's sit down and figure out what to do first," Toni said.

As she spoke the words, Brent came out of the kitchen in a navy blue robe, pajamas and slippers. The gorgeous Sunny from last night had morphed back into the dull-looking Brent. "Please, come in and have some coffee."

Then he looked behind Toni to her mom. "Linda, I think there's a spider on your cheek. And what happened to your eye? Did someone hit you?"

Linda put a hand up to the eye she'd poked herself in. "Do you have a bathroom I could use?"

"Yes, of course. Use mine. It's got the best lighting."

While Brent showed Linda to his bathroom, Toni led Tiffany into the kitchen and poured them both coffee. When they sat across from each other at the kitchen table, she said, "Okay. Tell me every single thing you can remember about last night."

"Like what?"

"What time did your father get home?"

She shook her head. "I didn't hear him. I was asleep."

"And what time did you go to bed?"

"Around midnight. I was waiting up for him, but I had my music on and I fell asleep with my earbuds in. He came in sometime after that, but I don't know when."

"Did the police say anything?"

"No. First, they asked if he knew Grant Forstman. And he said he did. Then they said they wanted to ask him a few questions down at the station. I did a Google search and found out that Grant Forstman was murdered last night."

"The cops must have given their names."

"They did but I don't remember what they were. It was all so awful."

"What did your dad say? How did he act?"

"At first he looked like he wanted to run away. I could see it in his eyes. He said he didn't know what they could want with a law-abiding citizen on a weekend morning and he'd better be back in time to make his daughter pancakes. Stuff like that."

Toni imagined he'd been babbling like a fool and Tiffany didn't know how to repeat all the stupid things he'd said without making him sound like an idiot.

"I don't know a lot about police procedure, but I don't think they arrested him. Did they Mirandize him?"

"Read him his rights?" Tiffany took a sip of coffee. "No. I don't think so. I'm scared, Mom. What are we going to do?"

She sipped coffee and then shook her head. "Honestly, I don't know."

"But you have to save him." She looked so young sitting there. "He's my dad."

Toni reviewed her options. Naturally, option Number One was to leave Dwayne D. Diamond in police custody so his time would be too occupied in saving his faithless butt to bother her or her daughter.

For several reasons, most of which concerned that daughter, she discarded option Number One.

Option Number Two was to try to find out whether Dwayne had been arrested and to see if she could get him out of jail.

When Linda arrived in the kitchen with Brent, who had changed into gray sweat pants and a white T-shirt, she said, "Mom, can you take over cooking breakfast? I've got to make a phone call."

"Please," Brent said, "allow me. I will make you my world-famous pancakes. I hope you like pancakes?"

She strongly suspected that they were going to taste exactly like the ones Dwayne had claimed he was going to make. It seemed Dwayne couldn't get close to anyone without trying to steal something from them. Their heart, their virtue, their daughter. In Brent's case, it seemed it was a purloined pancake recipe.

While the three were busy in the kitchen, Toni took her cell phone out front and settled in the velvet divan, which enfolded her with so much luxury she could imagine for a moment she was at the spa waiting for some delicious treatment to begin.

She selected the number on her phone and pushed send.

"Hey, Toni, what's up?" Luke had answered on the first ring.

"You didn't bark Marciano at me like you usually do," she said.

"You're a woman with personal problems. I was being sensitive."

"Don't let that story get around or you'll lose your rep as a ruthless cop."

"I take it you found her okay."

"Yeah. I did. Thank you for giving me the address."

"You don't sound like you're going to be on the next plane. What's going on?"

Sometimes it was spooky being involved with a man who saw what you tried to hide and heard what you didn't say. But sometimes it was wonderful. Depended on the situation.

In this one, having a man a step ahead of the obvious was a real bonus. "I need another favor." She let out a breath and decided to cut to the chase. "Dwayne's been picked up in connection with a murder. Tiffany won't leave until we figure out why and if there's a way to help him."

"Murder? That's pretty serious stuff."

"I know."

"Honey, if your ex-husband killed someone, he's in the right place. You have to let the cops do their job." He said it with an edge as though sometime in the past she might have been a little intrusive in an investigation he was involved in.

"Luke, I don't like Dwayne D. Diamond. I think he is a thieving, lying, cheating, heart-breaking, self-absorbed no good asshat. But I cannot believe Tiffany's father is a murder-er." She felt the weight of her daughter's trust that she could fix Dwayne's problems. "Worse, Tiffany doesn't believe it either."

"Poor kid."

"Yeah."

"Have you talked to him yet?"

"No. He was picked up about an hour ago. I want to know what they've got on him."

"You know that the critical time in a murder investigation is the first twenty-four hours. Evidence is fresh, witnesses are clear. Maybe they simply want to interview him."

"They hauled him down to the station rather than interview him at home. Why?"

He took a second to answer. "Probably because they think he did it."

"Can you find out what that case is based on? Here's what I know." By the time she'd outlined for him the name of the victim and that Dwayne had not only been threatened and beaten by the man a day before the murder but had claimed to have a meeting with him the night he was killed, even she could see that things weren't looking too good.

Luke obviously shared her dim view of things. "If you find out he is guilty as sin? Then what?"

She tried to imagine that far ahead. "I guess I would hire a defense attorney, make sure he got a fair trial. For Tiffany's sake."

"I'll talk to my buddy. See what I can find."

"Thanks, Luke."

"Don't get your hopes up, Toni. Most people who get picked up for murder did murder somebody."

"I know."

"Hang tight. I'll find out what I can."

"Thanks, Luke."

"Oh, and Toni?"

"Yes?"

"Don't go sticking your nose in where it doesn't belong."

She ended the call and rubbed her nose reflectively. Her nose was a little on the large side. It was the beauty flaw she most struggled against. Other women might complain of bad skin or skimpy hair, thunder thighs or a short waist. For Toni her beauty challenge was her nose. She did her best to bring out her other features by wearing heavier eye makeup and brilliant lipstick to draw the eye away, but nothing but surgery would ever make it smaller.

Luke said he liked her nose. He said it gave her character. He also once said, when he was irked, that it was her face's way of warning everyone in her path that she was one nosy woman.

Right now that nose was tingling. It did that sometimes when she was thinking deeply, having a big idea, trying to sniff out a new recruit or, in this case, a clue as to what had really happened to Grant Forstman.

"Mom," her daughter called, ending her reverie. "Come and look at this."

Toni walked back into the kitchen. The smell of frying pancakes filled the air with a comforting aroma. Brent was at the stove, an apron covering him from neck to thigh. Linda was frying bacon in a second pan, her much more voluptuous form also clad in an apron.

Tiffany was sitting at the kitchen table with her laptop. Toni had hauled it with her, reminding her that she needed to keep up with her homework.

"Look."

Toni sat beside her daughter and read the latest news bulletin that was up on the screen. "The details of the murder are already on the Internet?" she asked, continuously surprised at how fast bad news traveled in the digital age. The site was called Vegas News Underground and the post mixed fact with speculation and editorial comment. She doubted Vegas News Underground complied with the highest journalistic standards, but it was all they had to go on.

Under a flashing slogan that said "Breaking News" was this:

Casino Boss Found Shot to Death

The Double Nugget's owner, Grant Forstman, was found dead this morning in his office at the casino. Sources say an associate of Forstman found the body, which had been shot at least twice. Forstman, a frequent sight in the Double Nugget, was rarely seen without one of his two bodyguards.

Police removed security footage and have only said they have a person of interest in custody.

Our sources say Dwayne Diamond, a second-rate country and western singer who was appearing in the Double Nugget Show Lounge, is that person of interest.

Forstman leaves behind a widow, his third wife, Loretta Forstman.

Police have refused to comment on the case, but sources close to the slain man say Diamond and Forstman were seen arguing the night before the murder.

KEENLY AWARE THAT Tiffany was watching her read the report, Toni tried to put a positive spin on things. "This is all circumstantial, honey. He was seen arguing with the man. That doesn't mean he killed him."

"Are they going to let him out?" Tiffany asked. "When can I see him?"

"I don't know. Luke's going to find out what he can, and once we have some real facts, we can figure out what to do next." She patted her daughter's knee. "First, let's eat. These pancakes smell amazing."

In spite of her soothing words to Tiffany about waiting, Toni had never been one to wait around for things to happen.

The scent of a murder investigation would grow cold fast. While she waited for Luke to fill her in on the official facts, she decided to take a leaf out of Las Vegas Underground News's book and do a little unofficial digging of her own.

The problem was that her daughter, who usually went to incredible lengths not to be around Toni, was going to want to shadow her as she tried to help Dwayne. She needed to nip that in the bud.

So, while they ate pancakes that were, indeed, among the best she'd ever eaten, and everyone but her vegetarian daughter munched on bacon, she said to Tiffany, "I've got some work to catch up on back at the hotel. While I'm gone, you can work on your math assignment for next week."

Her daughter regarded her with suspicion. "How do you know I have a math assignment?"

"Please. Your generation did not invent email. We had it first."

The look her teen sent her was dripping with disdain. "Email? Who uses email anymore?"

"Your math teacher. Luckily. I contacted all your teachers and said you'd be away for a few days and asked for your homework assignments."

"Mo-o-ther," her daughter moaned, putting her head in her hands. She was so busy being mortified that her mom had butted into her world that she didn't even question where Toni was going.

"I hate calculus. I don't even understand it."

Brent forked a pancake onto his plate and said, "I'm a CPA. I aced math." He shot Toni a look that was full of understanding. "I can help."

"Thanks."

Now all she had to do was fob her own mother off, but fortunately, Linda had a date with the three Chers. Not even a murder investigation was going to derail her from giving makeovers and hopefully selling some Lady Bianca products.

CHAPTER 8

Her capacity for family affection is extraordinary. When her third husband died, her hair turned quite gold from grief.

— OSCAR WILDE

*M*urder hadn't affected business at the Double Nugget, Toni noted as she walked into the casino from one of the big glass doors on the street. The one-armed bandits were still holding out greedy hands for more money from gamblers who hoped luck would be on their side. She walked past a line of five-cent machines and tried to imagine wanting to spend hours plugging nickels into a machine.

She walked aimlessly, picking up the atmosphere, noting some sort of chemical smell coming off the carpets that she assumed was disinfectant. At mid-day on a Saturday there wasn't much action at the craps tables. A small group filled out a couple of tables in the blackjack pits, while a dealer stood looking bored.

A group of guys who looked like they hadn't been to bed in a couple of days hung around the roulette wheel. They had the red-eyed look of the sleep deprived as they placed bets more, she thought, to be part of the group than that they had much interest in the outcome.

She took particular note of the employees and while she caught sight of a few with their heads together clearly gossiping, she could not have said there was an air of grief among the workers.

Naturally, the road signs pointing to restaurants and bars and the show lounge didn't offer a clue as to where Grant Forstman's office might be located. She skirted the edge of the casino and found a set of stairs that looked as though they didn't go anywhere interesting. On a hunch, she ran lightly up them. When she got to the top, a slight huffiness in her breath reminded her that she hadn't been to the gym in a few days.

She knew she was in the right area for the administration offices not only because there was a sign directing her to Human Resources/Hiring, but also because there was a small flurry of activity down at the end of a corridor. A young cop in uniform stood outside the open door of what must be Forstman's office.

Well, she'd come this far. Toni usually went through life pushing forward until someone stopped her. It worked well in sales. She tried not to let her own insecurities stop her and instead worked on the belief that every woman would be happier, better off and definitely better looking if she let Lady Bianca into her life. She waited to hear a definitive *No* before she gave up.

Sleuthing, she'd discovered, was the same. You asked

questions and pushed against barriers until you got answers or someone stopped you in your tracks. In her limited experience, both were equally valuable.

Stopping only to freshen her lip gloss and give her appearance a quick once over in her pocket mirror, she began walking purposefully down the hall. As she got closer to the crime scene, she knew she had the full attention of the young doorkeeper cop. She kept her attention on how long it took her to walk to the end of the corridor and how many offices she had to pass to get there.

Four offices, as it turned out.

From the open door she could see that Forstman's office was a large one. A big desk in some shiny dark wood faced the door. He would see anyone who came in right away then and he'd see them coming from a long way away if the door was open. "Help you, ma'am?" the young cop asked, sounding official and unfriendly.

"Why, yes." She smiled as though he were only one makeover away from hosting a Lady Bianca home party for all the cops in the precinct. "I write a blog on local crime. I was wondering if you could tell me what happened here."

"No comment."

She took a quick glance into the office. Crime scene techs were at work on fingerprinting. There was no sign of a fight and the way the body had fallen, based on the dark bloodstain she could see on the rich navy carpet, she thought he must have stepped away from his desk. Heavy leather furniture included a leather couch large enough for a big man to nap on. The heaviness of the room was not helped by dark wooden paneling on the walls or the strong but stale smell of cigars.

"He was a cigar smoker, I see," she said, trying to think of anything she could say that might get this guy to lighten up and answer a few questions.

"Cuban, and quite illegal, though you can't arrest him now," a rich, low female voice said from behind her.

As she turned, the cop said, "Mrs. Forstman. I'm not sure —um, your husband's body's already gone."

Mrs. Forstman looked as though she'd been a showgirl who caught the eye of the boss. She was about Toni's own age and wore a figure-hugging top that revealed a fortune's worth of suntanned cleavage. Toni strongly suspected she bore no tan lines anywhere. Her trousers clung to round hips and long, long legs that ended in stilettos.

Grant Forstman's widow wore the opposite to funereal black. She was clad entirely in white from the short fur jacket to the shoes. She also sported diamonds, big, shiny real diamonds that hung from her ears and glittered between her breasts and sparkled on her fingers. Her hair was a rich brown with caramel and cranberry highlights.

"Yes, I know," she answered the police officer. "It was just that...I didn't know what to do with myself."

"Mrs. Forstman," Toni said, "I am so sorry for your loss."

"Thank you. And you are?"

Extremely conscious that she'd told the cop a lie and didn't want to repeat it for Grant Forstman's widow, she said, "Is there somewhere we could talk?"

The woman gave her a quick once over and whatever she saw caused her to nod. "Of course." She stepped forward, farther than Toni'd been allowed to, and scanned the room. To the officer she said, "I have my cell phone with me, of course, if there are any other questions."

She turned and strode down the hall, her hips swaying and that mane of hair dancing to the same beat as Toni followed.

She led them to an elevator. "God, I need a drink. Will you join me?"

"Of course."

"There's something about finding out my husband was murdered that makes me crave a martini." She spread her hands as though she was about to share a secret. "So much more fun than a Valium."

When the elevator doors opened, she led the way once more. "We'll go to the bar we keep for the whales." At Toni's raised eyebrows, she said, "The high rollers. Not that there will be many at this time of the day. We should have the place to ourselves."

They walked through a hushed area where a small group of men and women played cards and sat at blackjack tables. She felt an air of seriousness all around her. A large security guy nodded at Mrs. Forstman. She nodded back and led the way past the high rollers. At the back of the room was a bar discreetly tucked away in an alcove.

The walls glowed a deep green from glass panes lit somehow from behind. One entire wall was an aquarium full of exotic fish that emphasized the impression of being underwater.

Loretta sat them at a small table in the corner, and the single bartender who'd been lounging behind the bar when they walked in sprang to attention. He sped over to the corner table. "Mrs. Forstman. Please accept my condolences. How can I help you?"

"Thank you. I would like a Stoli on the rocks with a twist." She raised her eyebrows at Toni.

Knowing she couldn't attain intimacy with this woman if she drank soda, Toni asked for a vodka tonic. It was barely noon. She only hoped the pancakes would sop up some of the alcohol.

When their drinks arrived, Loretta Forstman took a grateful gulp then placed her glass on the table with a tap. "You said you wanted to speak to me? How can I help you?"

"My name is Toni Diamond."

At the sound of her name, Loretta's dark brown eyes widened and her head jerked slightly. "Diamond? As in Dwayne Diamond?"

"He's my ex-husband. Long time ago ex. Do you know him?"

The woman took another sip of her drink. Motioned the bartender for another. "Of course I know him. He works— worked for my husband. He is one of the acts in the show lounge."

A beat passed. Toni sipped her own drink. "He's also accused of your husband's murder."

"Look. I'm sorry about that. I don't know what you want with me."

"Neither do I," Toni answered honestly. "It's not me, it's my daughter. She's Dwayne's daughter too. She wants to find out what she can about the murder. See if there's anything we can do."

Loretta Forstman fished a pack of cigarettes out of her white leather designer handbag. She ripped the cellophane off the package. "I haven't smoked a cigarette in five years." She shook her head. Opened the package and pulled out a single cigarette with long, French-manicured fingers. There was a single package of matches in an ashtray in the middle of the table. The matchbox was rectangular. Like a coffin, Toni thought idly. The woman struck a match and lit her cigarette, then dropped the package into her purse. She took a long, luxurious drag of her cigarette, leaning her head back and closing her eyes. "You never lose the longing. Never."

She looked over at Toni once more. "You ever smoke?"

"No, thank goodness."

"So, Dwayne has a daughter. How old is she?"

"Sixteen. Her name's Tiffany."

The woman smiled. "Tiffany Diamond. Nice. She could get a job here in Vegas without having to think up a new name."

"How did you meet your husband?"

The woman took another long drag, as though she were kissing a long-lost lover. "Exactly the way you think I did. I was working—not here, on the strip. And Grant came in one night. He watched the show. He hired me to work in the Double Nugget. He said he fell in love with me from the legs up."

"How long were you married?"

"Almost four years."

"How did you find out your husband was, you know, dead?"

"The police came to the apartment around nine this morning. They told me."

"Apartment?" Toni had pictured Mr. Bigshot and his third missus in a mansion somewhere.

"We live upstairs. Grant never wanted to be away from this place. He was a workaholic."

"Weren't you already pretty worried? I mean, he didn't come home all night."

Loretta sent her a glance that spoke of long experience with a certain kind of man. "Toni, I was his third wife. Let's just say if my husband didn't come home once in a while, I wasn't going to make a federal case out of it."

"Did he make a habit of not coming home?"

"You mean was he seeing someone seriously?" She sipped her drink. "I don't think so. He was busy with work and I kept him satisfied at home. Like I say, it was the odd night he didn't come home. I didn't get too worked up."

She could dance around all day or she could cut to the chase. "The police have Dwayne in custody. Do you have any idea why Dwayne would kill your husband?"

"Toni. Do you really want to do this? Dwayne's a big boy who made some big mistakes. Let the law handle it."

"Oh, believe me, I'd love to. I want to tell my daughter something that makes sense."

Loretta stubbed out the remains of her cigarette. "No. I can't think of a reason why your ex-husband would kill my husband. Really."

"Loretta, my daughter was with her dad when your husband deliberately crashed into his car and then had two of his, um, associates, rough him up a little."

Her eyes widened in what looked to Toni like genuine surprise. "I didn't hear about that. He did that in front of your kid? Oh, my God. I'm sorry." She pulled out the pack of cigarettes again. Contemplated and dropped it back into her bag. "Look. Everybody likes Dwayne. He's easygoing and always has a joke or a compliment."

"My daughter heard Grant say, 'You have something that's

mine and I want it back.' Something like that." She watched the woman's face. "Do you have any idea what he was referring to?"

Her second martini arrived and Loretta sipped it before answering. "No idea."

"Any idea why your husband was meeting Dwayne last night?"

The other woman shrugged. "Dwayne may have wanted to make CDs? Advance his music career? I don't know."

Toni pulled one of her business cards out of her bag and passed it to her companion. "If you think of anything that might help us make sense of what's going on, would you call me?"

"Yes, sure," she said, picking up the card. Then she laughed. "Oh, my gosh. You sell Lady Bianca?"

"I sure do."

"I used to love that stuff. I lost my supplier when she moved out of state. Never bothered finding another one."

Toni didn't waste a nanosecond. "I'd be happy to offer you a makeover and show you our new line. I think you'll love the latest colors. There is a brand new selection of moisturizers full of botanical herbs and minerals from the Dead Sea that I swear by."

The woman nodded slowly. "I think a woman who just found out she's a widow deserves a makeover, don't you?"

"Yes, ma'am." Neither of them mentioned that the person giving the makeover was the ex-wife of the accused murderer.

"If you give me your number, I'll call you to set up a time for a makeover," Toni said, pulling out her cell phone.

Once she had the number punched in, she rose. Loretta

stood at the same time. Impulsively, Toni stepped forward and hugged the new widow. "I'm so sorry."

After a stunned moment, Loretta hugged her back. "Thank you."

She pulled away. "If there's anything I can do."

"I'll let you know."

As Toni walked away, she held the scent of Loretta Forstman's perfume. It was strong and spicy. And she'd smelled it before.

When her ex-husband had been leaning in trying to kiss her, she'd smelled that scent on him. In her experience with Dwayne, there was usually only one reason why he smelled of another woman's perfume.

CHAPTER 9

If I were asked to name the chief benefit of the house, I should say the house shelters daydreaming.

— GASTON BACHELARD

When Toni arrived back at Brent's house, she walked in to find *The King and I* playing on the big-screen TV. Deborah Kerr was singing "Getting to Know You," and Linda was humming along.

"Hi, y'all," Toni called out. Four heads turned her way. Linda and all three of the Chers had thick face masks on. And Japanese kimonos. "You look like a group of Kabuki actors," she said.

"Come join us, honey. I've got one more sample pack. It's the chamomile and French mud relaxation and exfoliating mask."

"Oh, I'd love to," Toni said. Her skin cried out for calmness and exfoliation after the dry air of the casino, the alcohol, the cigarette smoke. "But I can't right now."

"Maybe later," Linda said. And all four heads turned back to the television.

In the kitchen, she found her daughter and Brent practicing some horrendously complicated looking equations on foolscap. "Are you designing a space shuttle?" she asked, looking at the squiggles.

"No. Nothing so exciting. It's calculus."

"Oh." Toni'd never finished high school when she was supposed to, mainly because she met Dwayne and got pregnant with Tiffany. If those choices meant she'd never in her life learn calculus, she thought she could bear it.

"Have you heard anything from Dwayne?"

"No," Tiffany said.

"Does anyone have a problem if I go into Dwayne's room?"

"No," Brent said.

"Why?" asked Tiffany.

"I hope to find some kind of clue as to what's going on," she said.

"Do you want some help?"

"That's okay, honey. Wouldn't want to tear you away from the joys of calculus."

It felt strange entering Dwayne's bedroom. It certainly wasn't something she'd ever imagined doing again in her lifetime. It was even stranger knowing he was currently being held by police.

Dwayne had never been a particularly tidy man, and she saw that the last decade and a half hadn't changed him. It was easy to spot the clothes he'd worn last night as they were heaped on the floor. The jeans and the shirt that he'd worn to perform in were there. No doubt he'd put on another of his many pairs of jeans this morning for his ride to jail.

She picked up the shirt first. A whiff of Stetson hit her along with the meatier notes of cigar and the scent of Loretta's perfume clinging like gossip to a reputation. Her nose was pretty good but not good enough to distinguish whether the cigar she was inhaling now was the same as the one in Grant Forstman's office, but she felt it safe to assume it was.

Dwayne had never been a smoker. He refused to ingest anything that he thought might tamper with his golden voice. But he'd been around cigar smoke since this shirt had last been washed, possibly even smoked one in order to fit in. She picked up the jeans, went through the pockets. In one was a pack of the very same matches she'd seen Loretta Forstman use earlier to light her cigarette. They were the same oblong shape, embossed with the casino name. In the same pocket she found the gold label thingy from the cigar. Seemed he had smoked one, then, more worried about offending Grant Forstman, she wagered, than he was worried about damaging his vocal cords.

If she was right, and he'd smoked this cigar in Grant Forstman's office, she had to ask herself why. Why would he smoke a cigar with the man he was planning to kill? And why would Forstman offer a smoke to a man whose car he had deliberately damaged the day before?

She checked the rest of his room and didn't find anything of note. His laptop was old and as far as she could tell he only used it for email and for writing songs. His email was password protected. She knew enough about him that she could probably figure out his password if she had enough time. She doubted she had much time. If the cops arrested Dwayne they'd be right behind her, seizing his laptop and the clothes he'd worn.

A scatter of change sat atop his bureau. She went through his drawers methodically. Socks and underwear in the top drawer, a bowl of blue casino chips—she wondered if he got them as tips. A box of bolo ties and cufflinks. In the middle drawer were T-shirts, a pair of athletic shorts, sweaters. And in the bottom drawer, the jeans. She counted seven pairs of jeans, including a black pair and a white pair.

The pockets offered up receipts, crumpled notes with lines of songs scribbled on them, a few dollars, and some phone numbers. Always the phone numbers. Now, of course, they were cell phone numbers, and there was a scatter of email addresses in there as well. She couldn't imagine whispering to some guy, "Hey, why don't you email me sometime?" Maybe they were the married ones who didn't want to be bothered by phone calls.

In his closet was a collection of shirts. Denim ones, western formal wear with rhinestones, and the big belts. He owned a collection of boots, a pair of athletic shoes, and flip flops.

Nothing hidden under the mattress. Nothing in the room to explain what the hell her ex-husband had gotten himself into. A scatter of papers on his bureau included a checkbook with the edges curled. Statements and bills, some of which hadn't been opened. She took a quick look through his checkbook and the papers and got the strong feeling that Dwayne Diamond was having some money troubles.

She came out of Dwayne's bedroom with some thoughts, some scraps of paper with phone numbers, and some unwelcome memories. Some things never changed.

Tiffany looked heartily bored with math. She glanced up at her mother through thick lashes and put on her most charming expression. For a moment Toni felt like she was looking at a young Dwayne. Just for a second. And in that moment she remembered why she'd fallen for him.

"Mom, I really need a shower. Can I take a break?"

She tried not to appear as relieved as she felt. She'd been trying to figure out how to get her daughter out of earshot for a few minutes so she could ask Brent some questions. However, to avoid suspicion, she didn't give in right away. She turned to Brent. "What do you think? Has she learned anything?"

"I'd say we've made good progress. Tiffany's a very quick learner."

"Okay, then. You go shower up."

"And then can we see Dad?"

"I'll check with the police and ask when we can see your father."

As Tiffany left the room, she said to Brent, "And that's not a sentence you ever think you'll end up saying to your teenaged daughter."

"She's a great girl. I am really sorry she had to witness this."

He rose from the table and packed up his notes. Before he could leave the kitchen, she said, "Do you mind if I ask you a couple of questions?"

Brent's expression grew hunted. "Look, I really don't know him that well."

She smiled at him. "If it's women, please. We've been divorced forever. Anyway, it's not Dwayne's women I want to talk to you about."

He looked incredibly relieved. "Oh?"

"It's Dwayne's money."

Brent settled himself back into the chair he'd only just vacated. "Dwayne's money," he said slowly, as though those two words didn't belong next to each other.

"When's the last time he paid you rent?"

He adjusted his glasses and gazed at her for a long moment. Finally, he said, "He is a little behind on rent."

"Why do you let him stay?"

"Dwayne got us the gig at the Double Nugget. He introduced me to Grant Forstman and got us an audition." He shrugged. "There isn't such a call for female impersonators as there once was in Vegas. We're grateful to have the work."

"Who else does Dwayne owe money to?"

"Honestly, I wouldn't know. But he's got a lot of friends and everyone knows he'll pay up when he gets some money."

Then, she thought, her ex-husband must have changed, but she didn't say so.

She didn't even know why she was asking. Dwayne's lack of financial stability probably had nothing to do with the casino owner's death.

"Dwayne wanted me to invest in some business proposition he was very excited about. Do you know what that was?"

"No."

Brent was a CPA who owned his own home. She suspected she was not the only one Dwayne had tried to wrest money from. "Did he try to borrow money from you?"

"Yes. He did. But I wouldn't even let him tell me what it was. Huge return, fast turnaround? I told him to put his money in the bank. It sounded like a scam to me."

She nodded. She'd said almost the same words to

Dwayne. Now she wondered how many other people had turned down her ex-husband. Of course, if Grant Forstman was one of them, she was only strengthening the case against Dwayne.

"If he asked both you and me for money, he must have asked Grant Forstman. He's probably the richest man Dwayne's ever come across."

"I wouldn't be too sure about that."

She was genuinely surprised. "What? Are you saying that Dwayne is hooked up with a lot of wealthy people here in Vegas?"

"No. I'm saying I'm not sure Grant had a lot of money to invest."

He spoke carefully, his tone measured. He'd picked up a pencil and was doodling on the paper with the calculus equations.

"But that casino alone must be worth a fortune."

Brent smiled and looked up. "You know what we sell here in Vegas, Toni? We sell illusions. Dreams. This town runs on greed and hope."

"I've walked through the Double Nugget. It seemed real to me."

"But is Forstman's ownership real?"

She felt a little the way she imagined her daughter did trying to struggle through calculus. "I'm confused."

"I am only telling you this in the faint hope that it might help Dwayne. Frankly, I doubt anything can help Dwayne, but in case it's useful, please understand I am telling you this in the strictest confidence."

"Of course," she said, snuggling her butt further forward

on her chair. There was something so delicious about hearing secrets.

"Shortly after we started performing at the Double Nugget, Grant found out I was a CPA. He hired me to do some work for him. On the side, hush-hush. He'd bet heavily on real estate and got caught in the crash. He borrowed money against the casino. More than he should have borrowed and from people that don't like it when you don't pay them back."

"You mean the mob?"

"I don't know for sure, but I suspect Russian mobsters."

"So, you think Grant Forstman owed a lot of money to gangsters and when he couldn't pay it they killed him?"

"No. Frankly, I think Dwayne killed Grant. But if I can help you throw some reasonable doubt around, I will. Forstman wasn't the nicest guy in the world. I don't think a lot of people will cry at his funeral."

"Not his wife, certainly," she said, recalling her meeting with Loretta.

"You met Loretta?"

"Yes. We met at the casino today. I went over there to see if I could find out anything and we got to talking. She seemed nice. Levelheaded."

"Yes. Yes, she is." He suddenly stood up. "Well, I'd better get going or I'll miss my makeover."

She let him get halfway across the kitchen then, making sure she could still hear the shower going, said, "Brent?"

He turned. "Yes?"

"How long have Dwayne and Loretta been having an affair?"

His face scrunched up like somebody was threatening it with a fist. "How did you know about that?"

"I guessed. Thanks for confirming."

He sighed and shook his head. "It was supposed to be a big secret. I told him he was asking for trouble. I mean, come on, the boss's wife? But Dwayne didn't listen."

"How long had the affair been going on?"

"I don't know. A few months?"

"Did Grant Forstman know?"

"I thought you were trying to clear Dwayne?"

"I will if I can, but I need to know the truth."

"Did the man Dwayne is accused of murdering know that Dwayne was having an affair with his wife?" He nodded. "Yes. He did."

SHE'D DECIDED to wait until she heard from Luke before trying to see Dwayne since she needed to know exactly what their case against him was. So, as she was headed back to the hotel, she was relieved when her cell phone rang and Luke's photo came up. Every time she looked at the candid she'd snapped of him, it made her smile. She pulled over and answered. "Hi, Luke."

"How's it going down there?"

"Interesting."

"It's about to get a whole lot more interesting."

"Oh. You talked to your buddy?"

"Yes. You alone?"

"I'm in my car. Alone. I was going back to the hotel. Mother needs more Lady Bianca sample packs."

There was a short pause. "Right. Not even murder stops you girls shilling your makeup, does it?"

"Believe it or not, a little cosmetics party can give everybody a break from the grimness of a murder investigation. Also, it's amazing what people reveal when you have them in your hands. You'd be surprised."

"Having seen you at work, I would not be."

She thought there might be a back-handed compliment under the heavy layer of sarcasm, but she decided not to press the matter.

"Okay. I've got my notepad out. What have you got for me?"

"Toni, they can put him at the scene. He was seen entering Forstman's office on surveillance video. And he was seen leaving after midnight. No one else comes in until the morning when one of his henchmen shows up and finds the guy dead."

"That's bad."

"There were witnesses to an altercation he had the day before, but you know that because your daughter was there."

She scribbled notes as she talked. "Do they know Dwayne was having an affair with Loretta Forstman?"

"You beat me to the punchline. How the hell do you know that?"

If she told him she'd been snooping, he'd yell at her. She said, "It was a hunch."

She tapped her pen on her paper. The cops always approached crime from who was the most likely to have committed it. But her take was different. If she was bone-deep certain that Dwayne was incapable of murder, then she had to look at other approaches. Like, if he didn't do it, then who did?

"I heard that Grant Forstman always had one or both of his hired muscle with him. Where were they when Dwayne had his meeting?"

"One of them was sick with food poisoning. The other, Milos Karank, was there at the start of the meeting. The surveillance camera shows him walking away and down the hall around eleven forty-five."

"Why would he leave? That doesn't make sense."

"He's the one who roughed your ex up the day before. Maybe there was some delicacy involved."

She snorted. "Nothing about Forstman or his tough guys looked delicate to me."

"Toni, it doesn't matter why the guy left. The fact is that he did, and he didn't go back until the next morning. Dwayne Diamond was alone with Grant Forstman and then killed him."

"Over Loretta?"

"How do I know why he killed him? All I know is the facts are speaking pretty loudly and they're saying twenty-five to life." She'd done a little of her own research on the Internet. Nevada was a death penalty state.

"What about gunpowder residue? Did they find any?"

"No. But he could have worn a jacket he later threw away. He could have slipped on surgical gloves or scrubbed up thoroughly when he got home. Any fool with cable TV knows how to shoot someone and avoid gunpowder residue."

"I keep telling you, Dwayne's not that smart."

"Toni, how do you explain the surveillance tapes?" He was doing his best to be patient with her, but she could hear the sharp note. He was convinced Dwayne had done the deed and clearly believed she was wasting her time.

She thought about it. "I have cable TV too. They can be tampered with."

"They weren't tampered with. We have experts."

A couple of kids walked by, sullen teens. One was chewing gum like it was taking every bit of his attention; the other was moving his head in time to whatever he was listening to through his earphones. Those kids probably had normal lives, parents who worried about them. Dads who weren't in jail. "What can I do?"

"Seems to me he's a guy who has it coming. My advice is to get on the first plane and get back here."

"If it wasn't for Tiffany, I probably would. But I don't want her to grow up believing her dad is a murderer."

"Tiffany is a smart, stable girl. She'll find a way to deal with it."

Tiffany had only met her father a few days ago. She did not want the poor kid having to deal with him being a killer unless it was absolutely, positively certain it was true. "When can I see him?"

"They're not letting anyone see him except his lawyer until the bail hearing Monday morning. You can see him after that."

"A bail hearing? But that means—"

"It means that about thirty minutes ago your ex-husband was formally charged with murder."

CHAPTER 10

Sex is like money; only too much is enough.

— JOHN UPDIKE

oni had no idea what to wear to a bail hearing since she'd never been to one, but her usual policy every day was to dress as though something wonderful was going to happen.

So she put on one of her favorite dresses in blues and purples, slipped into heels and stuffed a sweater in her bag in case the air conditioning was too cold. Her makeup and hair were flawless, and she made certain to have a healthy stash of sample packs and her business cards offering free makeovers. She imagined a lot of people would hang around at court-houses with time to kill. Including her.

Talking about makeup and beauty routines would help brighten all their days.

Tiffany had slept over with them at the hotel on the pullout couch. They'd tried to pretend they were having a fun, girls' weekend away but underneath was always the knowledge that Dwayne was spending his weekend in jail.

"Can I come, Mom?" Tiffany asked, as Toni was deciding between diamond drop earrings or studs.

"No, honey. A courthouse is no place for you. Work on some more calculus or get started on your history project."

Her daughter threw her head back and made a sound of intense frustration before stomping off to the bathroom and slamming the door. "As if she was at home," Toni said to her mom. "For which I apologize."

"It's her father. Of course she's upset." Linda said. "Don't worry, honey. I'll look out for her. I was thinking we could go shopping or get our nails done."

When Toni arrived at Clark County Courthouse, she was very glad she'd worn bright colors, especially when she got to the courtroom where the bail hearing would take place. If the people sitting in the gallery weren't already depressed because of their loved ones being in trouble, looking around at all the black and navy, the droopy fabrics, pale faces and unkempt hair would make them so.

She was doing a little friendly fishing, chatting to a woman who sat near her to pass the time. When the woman's drug-dealing son made bail, she congratulated her and said, "Here's a little gift from me to you. If you want to give yourself the gift of looking better, give me a call," and she pressed the sample pack and her card on the stunned-looking woman.

As she moved to let the woman slide past her, she noticed her mother and daughter coming toward her. Tiffany said, "Mother, you did not seriously try to flog cosmetics to a woman who just bailed her son out of jail?"

"Name me one time when a woman wouldn't feel better if

she looked better?" Toni challenged. Then, realizing that both her daughter and her mother had turned up at the bail hearing, she snapped, "Anyway, that's beside the point. What are you doing here?"

"She threatened to hitchhike if I wouldn't bring her," Linda said.

"Hitchhike?" Had she taught her daughter nothing?

Tiffany fiddled with one of her silver rings. "The bus would have been too slow."

"I got us a cab," Linda said. "I figured if I came with her it would be better."

Toni had a choice. She could read her daughter a lecture or she could accept that the poor kid was worried sick about her father. She shuffled over a couple of seats to where the drug-dealer's mother had been sitting. "I'm really glad to have the company." She put a hand on Tiffany's and gave it a squeeze. To her surprise, her daughter squeezed back.

When Dwayne was called, he came out looking pale and shorter, somehow, as though being accused of murder had shrunk him. The navy blue jumpsuit hung on him. He glanced around, looking apprehensive, and when he spotted the three of them, he gave his best attempt at his usual cocky grin. She thought he'd have waved if he hadn't been handcuffed.

He was a no-good, morally corrupt man in so many ways, but Toni still couldn't believe he was a murderer.

The prosecutor, however, didn't seem to share her belief. The case was read out briefly, and the prosecutor wanted bail set at half a million dollars.

The defense attorney, who had briefly conferred with her client, said, "My client has family in the area and no reason or opportunity to flee. He does not have the financial resources to raise five hundred thousand dollars. We request a fifty-thousand-dollar bail, your honor."

The judge glared first at the lawyer and then at Dwayne, then snapped, "Bail is set at two hundred and fifty thousand dollars."

He glanced back at Toni once more as he was escorted by two courtroom deputies to a side door in the courtroom. She knew from chatting to the drug dealer's mother that the door led to underground access back to the jail. After Dwayne was gone, they called the next case, and Toni and her mother and daughter walked out into the hall.

"A quarter of a million dollars?" Linda said. "Where's he going to get that kind of money? He'd have to borrow fifty cents if he wanted to make a phone call."

"He can't raise it. He'll have to wait in jail for his trial." She was sorry for him, but not sorry enough to raise that kind of money for bail. Luke had said he'd try to get her an interview with Dwayne as soon as the bail hearing was over. She led them toward the exit so she could turn her cell phone back on.

"Wait," Tiffany said. "I'll put up the money I have in the bank from babysitting and birthdays and Christmas." She shot a pleading glance at Toni. "And I want to put up my college fund." Even as her mother opened her mouth, she said, "I keep telling you I don't want to go to college. Besides, it's like insurance. When he gets to trial without running away, we get out money back."

"You can't risk your college fund, sweetie."

"I'll put up my house," Linda said.

Toni and Tiffany both stared at her.

"I know, I like Dwayne about as much as I'd like a boa constrictor to climb into bed with me, but he is Tiffany's father and—well, that's all."

Toni shuffled her free makeover cards as though she were getting ready for a hand of poker. Her mother's mobile home wasn't worth anything like a quarter million. She thought of all the hours she'd worked her tail off to buy a house so Tiffany would grow up with a stable home.

Her daughter was looking at her with pleading eyes. She drew in a breath, let it out again. "I'll put up my house as collateral." And, she thought, if Dwayne let her down again she'd be the next one standing trial for a murder. His.

Tiffany hugged her. She hugged back.

"I'm going to have to go and fill out paperwork and so on, for the bond. Why don't you two go shopping? There are great outlet malls near here. We can meet up later."

The two seemed relieved to be heading out of this depressing place and who could blame them? She'd like to be out of here herself. But first, she had to put the home she'd worked so hard for in jeopardy for a man who didn't deserve any help. Then, she was really hoping she could see him. Not because she wanted to be up close and personal with Dwayne Diamond, but because she had some very pointed questions to ask him.

Two hours later, Toni sat across from her ex-husband in an airless room with bars on the windows. She was in the visitors' facility in the jail. Not somewhere she'd ever imagined herself.

Apart from seeing him perform at the club and have him try to wheedle money out of her in the parking lot, she hadn't seen Dwayne in more than sixteen years. She realized how far she'd come from the young girl who'd been fooled by his good looks and smooth-talking lies.

She was a different woman now, but she quickly realized he was the very same man. Still thinking that good looks and smarmy charm could get him anywhere.

"Honey," he said, his tired face lighting in a big grin when she walked into the interview room. "I knew I could count on you. I knew my smart, successful wife would get me out of this jam."

"I'm not your wife anymore, Dwayne." He always smelled so good, like sex and Stetson cologne. But now he smelled stale.

"But neither of us have ever married again. That has to count for something, right?"

If she hadn't heard the edge of desperation in his voice she would have let him have it, but she could tell he was terrified. And with good reason.

A quick glance showed her where the surveillance cameras were, one pointing at her, one at Dwayne. She knew from Luke that there was also audio surveillance. She pulled out her notebook and pen.

"Cut the crap, Dwayne." Then she leaned in and lowered her voice. "Tell me everything and it had better be the truth."

He sat across from her looking a little lost without his usual props, his tight jeans and cowboy shirts, his big hats and the show-offy boots. The navy jumpsuit and handcuffs was not a good look on him.

"I didn't kill Grant. I swear to God."

"Then why do the cops think you did?"

She clicked open her pen. Not that she really intended to

take notes but she thought it would make Dwayne more businesslike if she was, too.

He dropped his gaze to the scarred tabletop and shifted as though he wanted to use his hands and couldn't. The gesture made him look so unsure of himself that in spite of herself, she softened. This was Tiffany's father, after all. She gentled her tone. "I can't help you if you don't tell me everything."

He glanced up, hopeful, eager. "You don't think I killed a man, do you?"

"It looked to me like you have a good lawyer who will do everything she can to help you."

He scowled. "She said she was hiring a defense investigator. But he's tied up working another murder case that's in trial right now. He won't be able to work on my case for at least a month." He looked amazed that any case could be more urgent than his. "You've gotta help me."

"I am prepared to listen to your story. I don't believe the man I once loved would be capable of murder, but then I didn't think he'd dump me with a baby and leave town, either."

He blew out a breath. "They took my fingerprints and mug shots. Treated me like a criminal."

"They caught you on a surveillance camera, leaving Grant Forstman's office right around the time of his murder. No one else went in or out until he was found dead the next morning right in that office." She kept her voice low and after a quick glance at the cameras, he did the same.

"He was alive when I left him. You have to believe me!" He looked terrified, desperate, but also truthful. Toni'd heard so many of his lies that she was pretty good at reading him. "You posted bail. Why aren't I getting out?"

"It has to be processed. They're putting a lien on my house. I don't think you're going anywhere for a couple more days."

He sank down like a man-shaped balloon with the air seeping out.

"You and Grand Forstman argued the day before he was killed and his hired muscle beat you up. Then you had a cozy meeting in his office? What am I missing?"

"I borrowed some money from Grant," he murmured at last.

She was so startled she dropped her notebook to the table. "The guy I saw at the casino did not look like a man who lends money without some hefty collateral."

Dwayne fidgeted on the hard chair. "He didn't exactly know I borrowed it."

"You stole money from a gangster?"

"No! I told you, I borrowed it."

"How did you come to borrow it?"

He flicked a glance at her face and down again. "This deal was a no-brainer. I went to Forstman for a loan and he turned me down flat. So I borrowed the money. Figured I'd pay it back as soon as I could."

"But he found out."

He nodded, swallowing hard.

"And you went to see him because?"

"He said he wanted to see me after the show. The guy was my boss, what could I do? So I went up there."

"And?"

"He wasn't happy, but he's a businessman. He said I had exactly three days to return the money. With hefty interest."

"What did you say?"

He looked at her as though that was a really dumb question. "I told him I'd get it, of course."

"And where were you going to get the money?"

His gaze dropped. "I had some leads."

"Like trying to extort money from me using my daughter as collateral."

"She's our daughter. And can't a man get to know his little girl without his ex-wife making a federal case out of it?" But his words sounded so weak she didn't bother arguing.

"Speaking of federal cases, you are charged with murder. Let's get back to the details of your meeting with Grant Forstman."

"I told him I'd have the money back in three days. End of story."

"How much money are we talking about?"

"Thirty grand."

Thirty thousand dollars was definitely enough money to beat a guy over. But was it enough to kill for? "What did you need the money for?"

"A business proposition. I told you. Can't lose. But the capital's invested right now. That's why I was hoping you'd be my investor instead of him." He cracked a weak grin. "You're a whole lot better lookin' than Grant."

She leveled her gaze on him. "And that was the extent of your meeting?"

"Yes. We even smoked a cigar together." His gaze dropped to the notebook she had out on the table. And then she got it. Forstman had all but pushed Dwayne into smoking a cigar, knowing how much her ex-husband hated smoking. He was making the point that he pretty much owned Dwayne.

"So, you smoked a cigar together and you walked out of there?"

"Sure. He was real clear. I had three days and if he didn't get the money, something bad would happen to me."

"Worse than your car getting cracked up and you getting beat up?"

He nodded, still not looking up. "He said that was a warning."

"What happened to the guy who beat you up?"

"He patted me down when I got to the office. I was clean and Grant told him to go home. His partner was sick, and he looked kind of green. Grant has a thing about getting sick." He gulped. "Had a thing about getting sick."

"How long was your meeting?"

"Not long. He made me wait before he could see me. We were together maybe fifteen, twenty minutes?"

"And when you left, he was fine."

"Yeah. I told you."

"What was he doing?"

"Huh?"

"When you left, what was he doing? Packing up to go home? Sitting behind his desk? Picking up the phone? What?"

"Oh. I get you." He turned to look out the window, saw bars and jerked his head back again so he was looking at her once more. "He was sitting behind his desk. I walked out and I think I heard the phone ringing."

"You think the phone was ringing?"

"Yeah."

"Dwayne, this is really important. If you didn't kill Grant then the person on the phone could have been the killer."

"Oh, right. I never thought of that."

That's because you think with your dick. He closed his eyes and she gave him time.

"Yeah, the phone was definitely ringing."

"Did you hear him say anything?"

"Hey, baby."

"Hey, baby? You're sure?"

"Pretty sure."

"Dwayne D. Diamond, if you are making this up in a feeble attempt to get out of a murder charge, I have to tell you that wasting my time will do the opposite."

"No. I mean, I really did hear him say 'Hey, baby,' I didn't think of it till now, is all."

"Who was the *hey, baby* in his life?"

"His wife, I guess."

"Loretta?"

"Yeah. Loretta."

A beat passed. The air smelled stale and in a corner a fly was buzzing.

"How did you borrow the money?"

"What do you mean?"

"Do not play dumb with me. I'm guessing he doesn't keep thirty grand lying around on his desk."

She could tell he was about to lie and then even he must have realized that telling her the truth was his only hope of getting out of a murder charge. He slumped a little. "I took it from his safe."

"And how did you get into the safe?"

"I had the password."

"Grant Forstman gave you the combination to his safe?"

"No. I, ah, I found it." He looked to the door as though

someone would come rescue him from this conversation. It didn't happen.

"Where did you find the combination to his safe?"

"I need some water. My throat's dry." He glanced at the door once more. "Do you think you could get me some water?"

"Where did you find the combination to his safe?" She resisted yelling *lunkhead* in his face, but only barely.

"People are so careless with those things. It was written down on a paper in his wallet. He left his wallet at the club one night. I copied down the number. He never knew anything about it."

She let a beat pass.

"Who do you think killed him?"

He shifted on the hard chair like he ought to have a guitar in his hand and without it he didn't know how to sit still. "What?"

"If you didn't kill Grant Forstman, who do you think did?"

"How do I know? A man like that has enemies. He's rich, doesn't always treat people real good, I don't know."

She rose, thinking she had everything she was going to get out of Dwayne. "Okay. I'll be in touch."

"When do I get out of here?"

"I don't know."

"Toni," he said, desperation in every note. "I'm too good lookin' to go to jail."

CHAPTER 11

Half a truth is often a great lie.

— BENJAMIN FRANKLIN

The sun felt warm when she left the jail. She sat down on a bench, her head spinning. Visiting your ex-husband in jail will do that to a girl, she decided. A few couples wandered by, headed for the marriage bureau at the courthouse in the same downtown complex. And good luck to them. She needed a few minutes to collect her thoughts and go over everything Dwayne had told her. One big whopper lie stuck out like the nose on her own face, but otherwise, she felt Dwayne had told her the truth.

She did not believe he'd killed Grant Forstman.

He'd also not been able to shed any light on who had killed the casino owner.

She scribbled a few notes in her notebook. It was the kind of thing she sometimes did when she was searching for fresh ways to market Lady Bianca cosmetics. *Think outside the box*, she was always telling her girls.

This was a perfect example of a time to use that strategy. Dwayne had jammed himself into quite a box, but if he was innocent, then the real killer was out there and she had to look all the way outside that box to find out who it was.

She wrote the word *Sex* on a blank page and put two vertical lines through the S to make a dollar sign. Everything kept coming back to sex and money.

She retrieved her car and drove slowly back to Brent's place, where she'd agreed to meet up with her mom and her daughter so Tiffany could pick up some more of her clothes. She'd refused to pack everything, as though by leaving traces of herself in the house where he lived, she was somehow supporting her dad.

When Toni got there, only Brent was home.

"How did it go?" he asked.

She made a face. "About as well as can be expected when you're trying to get your cheating ex out of a murder charge."

"Want some tea? I was just going to make some."

"Tea would be wonderful."

They sat at the kitchen table and she asked the question that had plagued her since she left the jail. "Who gets Grant Forstman's money?"

Brent poured boiling water over tea bags in a teapot decorated like The Mad Hatter's Tea Party. He opened the fridge and pulled out milk, which he poured into a matching jug. The sugar pot was already on the table. "What do you mean?"

"If Dwayne didn't kill the man, and I don't think he did, then I have to figure out who did. Follow the money, honey."

He poured tea for both of them, then sat down slowly. "I'm not sure there is a lot of money."

She tapped the tabletop with her nails and caught the glitter of a fake diamond. "Like you said, Vegas is all about selling illusions. To the outside world he was a rich casino owner who would have been worth a fortune."

She sipped her tea, glad of its simple comfort.

"But he wasn't," Brent said. "And he was in big to some bad guys."

"I know. I mentioned that to my—" She never knew what to call Luke. "My friend who's a cop back home. He said the LVPD are looking into it. But, I don't see what Russian mobsters would gain by killing him." She thought about how Grant Forstman had roughed up Dwayne and threatened him to get his money back. She pretty much thought big-time thugs would act the same with Forstman, only on a larger scale.

"Does your friend think Dwayne is innocent?"

"No. But he's a cop. He tends to think the most obvious suspect did the deed. Usually, he's right."

"But not this time?"

"Maybe." She felt frustrated and edgy.

"Are you taking this so hard because he's Tiffany's father or because you can't accept that your judgment was so far off?"

She felt the sting of his words even though they were softly delivered. "Ouch. Maybe a little bit of both. Nobody wants to think they married a murderer."

"You were sixteen. What did you know?"

She smiled ruefully. "My mother's been talking. Hasn't she?"

"She loves you. And she's a very smart lady."

Toni blinked at him.

"Linda was absolutely right, the rash is clearing up on my chest."

She had to smile. She wasn't sure that prescribing a hypoallergenic moisturizer qualified her mother for Mensa, but it was nice that she was helping out while she was here. Already, Sunny and the Three Chers were sporting clearer skin and much better stage makeup colors.

Which wasn't going to get Dwayne out of trouble. She said, "Loretta was Grant Forstman's third wife. Does she get whatever there is? Are the exes in for a chunk? Kids?"

"Loretta has expensive tastes," he said.

She nodded, recalling the diamonds and fur coat. Even her hair coloring had to cost a fortune to maintain. "Poor thing. I wonder what she'll do when she finds out she's broke."

"More tea?"

"Hmm? No. I'd better not." She traced the Mad Hatter ceramic figure with a fingertip. "I keep searching for other suspects, but Dwayne sure does look guilty. He didn't even admit he was sleeping with Loretta. He thinks I don't know."

"But you don't think he killed Grant Forstman?"

"No. No, I don't."

"I hope not. For Tiffany's sake. She's a great kid."

"She sure is." She smiled. "She's probably the best thing Dwayne ever did in his life, and he doesn't even realize it."

He made a funny noise. "He's like a lot of men. Get a woman pregnant and they're out of there." He spoke with so much bitterness, she asked, "Is that what happened to you?"

Then she said, "I'm sorry. I speak first and engage my brain later. It's none of my business."

He shook his head. "It's okay. I never knew my father. He left my mother before I was even born. There's no one I admire more than my mother. She was a Vegas showgirl, too. My act's a kind of a tribute."

"That's wonderful. She must be so proud."

"She died a couple of years ago, but she got a real kick out of Sunny and the Three Chers. Some of the costumes I wear are hers. That was pretty much the bulk of her estate."

And here they were back at estates. "But you think Grant Forstman didn't have the money he appeared to have?"

He smiled slightly. "This is Vegas, Toni. Everything is built on fakery and pretense. In my professional opinion, that man was close to bankrupt."

"Poor Loretta." She pulled out her smartphone. "You know what every woman needs when she's feeling a little down?"

He looked at her with narrowed eyes. "A good friend with a bottle of scotch?"

She fluttered her lashes at him. "A new friend with unlimited makeup."

She swiped on fresh lip gloss, pulled up her smile and positive attitude and called Loretta's number. To her surprise, Grant Forstman's widow answered right away. "Loretta Forstman."

"Loretta, it's Toni Diamond, we met the other day at..." Usually she was smooth on the phone, but she had no way to finish that sentence without the words "murder" and "corpse" hanging in the air like skunk spray.

"The casino, I remember," Loretta said, seeming a lot more smooth than Toni. "What can I do for you?"

"I'm hoping I can do something for you." These were such familiar words that her patter unrolled ahead of her like a red carpet leading to Oscar night. "I would love to offer you a complimentary Lady Bianca makeover."

"Oh. I'm really not—"

"Please don't worry about wasting my time. I met you and liked you immediately. And after the horrible shock you've been through, you and your skin need some pampering."

"But your husband is accused of murdering mine. Isn't that kind of icky?"

"Please, Dwayne hasn't been my husband for fifteen years. That's half my lifetime." If you weren't very good at simple division.

"Well, I really did like Lady Bianca cosmetics when I used to wear them."

"Trust me, you are going to love the new line. I'm bringing some extra samples of the skin creams for you. Honestly, three months of using the new line and you'll feel like you've had a facelift. Without the stitches."

"If you're sure you don't mind."

"I don't at all. What time shall I come by?"

"You do it here?"

"Absolutely. We pay house calls like doctors and priests used to."

She was treated to a low, throaty laugh. "You'll probably do me more good than either of those."

They made a date for the next day. Toni would have kept chatting, but she had another call coming in.

"Toni Diamond," she trilled.

"Mom, you've got to get over here," Tiffany yelled.

"Where are you?"

"At the Wentworth Casino."

"The Wentworth? What are you doing there?" The Wentworth was one of the top casinos on the strip, near the Bellagio.

"Grandma wanted to come. She thought it would make us feel better."

"I thought you were going shopping."

"We did. There's a huge mall here as well as the casino."

"And why do I need to get over there, right away?"

"Because Grandma got arrested."

CHAPTER 12

You have to learn the rules of the game and then you have to play better than anyone else.

— ALBERT EINSTEIN

"*W*hat?" She shrieked so loud that Brent spilled hot tea on his hand. "Grandma got arrested?" She could not take much more of this.

"Well, not arrested exactly. Hauled away by the security guys."

"Hauled away for what?"

"I don't know."

Toni was so stressed she grabbed at her hair, messing up the careful style she'd spent twenty minutes on this morning. "What's she done? She didn't get into a fight, did she?" Toni would never forget one memorable day when her usually happy mother all but ended up decking some woman who claimed that Dolly Parton could not sing a note.

"No. It wasn't a fight. I don't know. She was excited. She

loves the casino. She was playing roulette, and I think she was winning. A server brought her champagne and me a Coke. Then all of a sudden these two guys in black came up and said she had to go with them. Nobody will tell me anything. I'm not old enough to be in the casino, but they let me go. They took Grandma away somewhere."

"And where, precisely, are you at this moment?"

"I'm sitting in the ice cream parlor at the Wentworth."

"Okay. Don't move. I'm coming." Then, before the call ended, she said, "Wait, Tiff, what were you doing in the Wentworth?" There were a dozen casinos and places to shop that were closer.

"Dad gave me a couple of blue casino chips for the Wentworth before, you know, all the crap happened. He said to go and have some fun with them at the casino, but I don't like gambling. And I'm not supposed to be in the casino anyway, so I gave them to Grandma."

Toni closed her eyes. "I'll be there as quick as I can."

"Mom?"

"Yes, honey."

"What should I do?"

Toni knew what she'd like to do. "Order a hot fudge sundae. And tell them to make it a double."

When she got off the phone, Brent was looking at her with concern. She grabbed her bag. "Suddenly everyone in my family is a criminal."

She recalled from her quick search of Dwayne's room after he'd been arrested that she'd spotted a bowl of chips. She hadn't thought anything of them at the time, now she stopped to pick them up and count them. They were blue. Nothing about them suggested what each chip was worth, but there was a W embossed on each one. She borrowed a paper lunch sack from Brent and dropped the chips in it, then headed back out to her car. She need to spring her mother from casino jail.

~

WHEN SHE ARRIVED at the casino on the strip, she discovered that the Wentworth was to the Double Nugget what Paris, France was to Paris, Texas.

She pulled up to valet parking and a man dressed like something out of a Jane Austen movie rushed up and opened her door, holding out his hand as though he were Colin Firth himself. She took his hand and let him help her out of her car. He handed her a slip of paper and said, "Call when you're ready and we'll get your car for you right away, miss."

She slipped a twenty from her wallet and handed it to the young man, giving him a dazzling smile.

"Thank you." She squinted at his nametag, "Vernon." And she waltzed into the grand entrance of the hotel. Two more Georgian footmen rushed to open the opulent, heavy glass doors for her. Little did they know their security people had her mother in lockup.

Having used the time driving over to formulate some sort of strategy, she was certain of one thing. She needed Tiffany to stay put. She texted her daughter with a little white lie. *Traffic terrible. I'll be there as soon as I can.*

And then, trying not to look like a woman here to bail her own mother out of casino jail, she asked the first person she saw in uniform for directions to the casino security office.

"Casino security?"

"Yes."

"Go on through to the casino and ask one of the security people. They'll escort you up."

Toni headed for the casino. She had never in all her life seen so much crystal. Not that she'd ever had occasion to go to Paris, never mind Versailles, but she had a sense that Marie Antoinette and her court would be right at home here. The chandeliers alone were the size of small planets, sparkling and glittering above the heads of a pretty upscale looking crowd.

When she headed through all the glitz and glam, she paused at a roulette wheel. About eight people were playing and a few spectators watched idly. The chips looked exactly like the ones she'd found in Dwayne's possession right down to the W on each chip. Players had little piles of different colored chips in front of them. She spotted a couple of blue ones.

One man seemed to watch with more interest than the others, as though he might be thinking of joining the game. She sidled up to him. "Excuse me," she said. "Where do I buy chips?"

He pointed to the side of the casino where a counter ran along the wall. It looked like a bank with a series of tellers inside secure booths. "Thank you," she said. "Do you know what denomination the blue chips are?"

"Blue's five hundred bucks. But you can play at this table for five bucks. Better to start there," he said kindly. "Those chips are the white ones."

"I will. Thanks again." She walked away wondering what Dwayne was doing with ten grand worth of Wentworth casino chips. And why playing them had landed her mother in hot water.

Maybe she'd seen too many gangster movies, but before she got into the elevator that would take her to security and, she suspected, far from the glittery chandeliers and prettily dressed gamblers, she pulled out her cell phone and called Luke.

"Hey, pretty lady, what's up?"

In spite of her stress and worry, she felt a smile tilt her lips. "You miss me."

"I do not. I can watch football without someone asking me every five minutes who has the ball."

"Oh, so unfair. I don't care who has the ball. I always want to know when it will be over."

"Too true." He sighed. "I'm guessing you didn't call me to talk about football."

"No. Things are so bad here I actually wish I was sitting in front of a big screen with you watching a game I don't like and don't understand."

"That bad, huh?" And for Luke, that was like sending the mushiest sympathy greeting card ever written and imprinted with purple flowers.

"My mom's been nabbed at the casino for gambling with stolen chips."

"Your mom?"

"Yeah. I suspect she got the chips from Dwayne." She wanted to be tough and sassy but right now she felt a little bit wobbly. Like her stilettos were too high and she was about to fall flat on her face.

"Which casino?"

"The Wentworth."

"The Wentworth?" He sounded stunned. "They'll have state-of-the-art surveillance and top-of-the-line anti-theft programs. What kind of moron steals from the Wentworth?"

She sighed. "I believe I mentioned my ex-husband Dwayne Diamond may have been involved."

"What do you need?"

"You see? That's what I like about you. You're not warm and fuzzy, but you give practical help."

"Warm and fuzzy is for teddy bears. You need brass balls to get out of this jam."

"I don't have—"

"Sure you do. Well, brass ovaries anyway."

"You really think I do?"

"Honey, you could sell cosmetics to the Amish."

She knew he was making a joke, but personally, she'd always thought the Amish would be happier with cosmetics. The women would look so much prettier, and the men could take advantage of the men's skincare line. But now wasn't the time to get into that. "Okay, here's what I need. If you don't hear back from me in an hour, you know I'm being held at the Wentworth."

"Copy."

"It's not funny, Luke. Seriously, I'm worried."

"I doubt they'll take this to the cops. Your mom's not exactly a big threat. Play nice, tell them you'll never do it again and get the hell out of there."

"Okay. And if you don't hear from me in an hour?"

"I'll get hold of my buddy in Vegas. He'll get you out."

"Promise?"

"Yeah. And if he doesn't, I'll be on the next plane to take care of it myself."

"You don't have jurisdiction."

"I have a vested interest in a certain pushy Lady Bianca saleswoman."

"How vested?"

He chuckled, low in his throat. "When you get back to Texas, I'll show you."

She smiled. Even though her world felt as though it was falling to pieces, Luke still made her smile. "Deal."

The smile made it past the blackjack tables and a couple of craps tables to a dark-suited man with a badge on. "Excuse me. I'd like to go to security, please."

He stared at her as though this was the White House and she'd asked to see the President.

"What's your business with security?" He was polite, but unsmiling.

How to phrase this? "My mother's up there. I think there's been a misunderstanding."

He pulled out a cell phone. "Name?"

"Toni Diamond. My mother is Linda Plotnik."

He spoke in a low voice to someone and then said, "Come with me." He led her to an elevator at the back of the room and they stepped into it. It shot up and then the door opened. As she stepped out, she got a sense that in entering the security zone she was entering another world.

Confidence, she reminded herself as scary guy deposited her at a reception desk where a young woman who could probably break every bone in her body with an eyelash said, "Can I help you?"

If you truly believe you'll get what you want you're more likely to succeed, she reminded herself. She looked the woman in the eye, exuding confidence. "Yes. I'm looking for Linda Plotnik."

It was eerily like her visit with Dwayne earlier in the day. Once more she was shown to an airless, awful room that smelled like fear and smashed dreams. There was a desk, a phone, a couple of cheap office chairs. Not so much as a photograph on the walls or a potted plant brightened the atmosphere.

Her mother wasn't there, but a tough looking bald guy came in right behind her. He looked like all his body's resources went into building so much muscle that there was no energy left for anything as frivolous as hair.

"Your mom's in a heap of trouble," he said, looming over her and looking sinister.

It was funny. She'd been so nervous on her way here, but now that she stood in front of a guy who looked like he should be in a cage, her nerves were steady. She said, "So will you be if you don't release her immediately."

"Linda Plotnik was gambling with stolen chips."

She held her expression steady with an effort, but inside she was cursing Dwayne all over again. Stolen casino chips? What had he got himself involved in? "My mother had no idea. Those chips were given to her."

His eyes were cold and nasty. "Who gave her the chips?"

"I don't know." Little white lie number two in less than twenty minutes. "But my mother is no thief."

"They all say that."

"I doubt it."

"Think you're pretty tough."

"No. I think that legally you can't do anything. You haven't called the police, so I suspect you have nothing but a suspicious chip that somehow came into my mother's possession."

He leaned back, regarded her with something closer to respect. "Okay, you won't be bullied. I like that."

"Thank you."

"Here's the thing, Ms. Diamond. When people steal our chips, we don't like it. It's bad for our business, bad for our honest clients and bad for the reputation of Las Vegas."

"I can appreciate that."

"If we can get the name or names of the people who gave your mother the stolen chips, we could probably let her go, with a ban on ever playing here at the Wentworth again, of course."

"How many chips were stolen?"

"Ms. Diamond, please." He folded his arms over his massive chest.

"If I was able to return, let's say, ten grand worth of chips, do you think you could forget my mother was ever here?"

He stared at her out of eyes so cold a blue they ought to freeze over. Then gestured to her handbag. "Why don't you hand me over that nice bag, Ms. Diamond?"

"Have you never heard that a woman's handbag is one of her most private possessions?"

His smile was lizard-like. "Not when you're in my office."

"Well, I'm not giving it to you. You have absolutely no right to—"

"I've always preferred taking what I want." And he reached out and grabbed her bag.

She gave a cry of outrage as he snatched her beloved bright pink Kate Spade. To wrestle the man would not only be undignified but since he weighed about two hundred pounds more than she did and looked like he took part in extreme fighting when he was bored, she gave in.

He upturned her bag and out spilled her wallet, her cell phone, her diamond-encrusted eyeglass case, her notebook and pen, her makeup bag (the small one, for touch-ups), and a blue bag with no discernible purpose. He sent her a smug glance of triumph. "Now where would a nice lady like you hide stolen casino chips?" he asked as he reached for the blue bag.

She compressed her lips and then instantly relaxed them. She wasn't going to inflict premature wrinkles around her mouth for him. He unzipped the bag and turned it upside down. A cascade of Lady Bianca sample packs spilled onto the desk. "What the hell?"

"Sample packs of this season's Lady Bianca cosmetic line," she told him sweetly. "Please, help yourself."

With a scowl he went after her makeup bag. Out tumbled her mascara, a small eye shadow compact, lipstick, lip gloss and lip liner, a small tube of blemish concealer, and a slightly larger one of foundation. Face powder, blush, and a small spray bottle of Evian. He sprayed and sniffed at the resulting puff of moisture droplets.

"Evian. It's excellent for fighting dehydration of the complexion. You should get some. The casino air is very drying."

He put down the spray bottle with unnecessary force and shook out the rest of her bag. A couple of loose quarters fell out, a pack of tissues and a roll of mints. A discreet pouch that contained two tampons. He opened the pouch. Scowled. Shut it.

He glared at her. "Where are the chips?"
She glared right back. "Where is my mother?"

CHAPTER 13

Good people do not need laws to tell them to act responsibly, while bad people will find a way around the laws.

— PLATO

The standoff continued for thirty unnerving seconds. Finally, he made a growl like a cornered grizzly—or Tiffany when she didn't get her way, and stomped out of the small office. She rose and gathered her belongings back into her bag, then sat back down and waited, hoping she looked much calmer than she felt.

In a very short period of time, the door opened again and the thug pushed Linda into the room. "Oh, Toni," her mother cried. "I'm so sorry. I had no idea those chips were stolen."

She hugged her mother, who was so distraught one of hair extensions had come loose and she hadn't noticed. It hung from her head like an animal tail. "It's okay, Mom. Did they treat you okay?"

Her mother's eyes went squinty. "If you call getting

grabbed off the casino floor like a criminal and yelled at and threatened good treatment, then they treated me like a queen."

She squeezed her mother's shoulder. "Ready to go?"

"An hour ago."

"Okay." She turned to the security guy who stood blocking the door out of there. "I will return the chips if you tell me exactly what you know of the theft. And, naturally, there will be no further unpleasantness toward my mother."

He glared some more. She glared back some more.

"Wait here."

Like they had a choice. He disappeared and in a couple of minutes more, a different man entered. A man different in every way. He wore a decent suit, flashed a smile so dazzling you could use the reflection to apply eyeliner, and smelled like expensive cologne.

"Ladies," he said, as he walked in on shiny loafers. "I understand you have information that could help us recover some stolen property." He walked forward, shook hands first with Toni, then Linda. "I'm Nathan Chisolm, head of security here at the Wentworth." He glanced around the grim room as though he'd never seen it before. "Please, come into my office."

He led the way and as they followed, Linda whispered, "Good cop, bad cop?"

Toni glanced back and nodded. But bad cop had also boosted them up the chain of command. Besides, she liked Nathan Chisolm's manners much better. His office was down the hall and around a corner. It was large and well furnished, seeming to belong to the Wentworth. He gestured to a round glass table with half a dozen comfy chairs gathered around it. "Please, have a seat."

Toni and her mother sat side by side and he settled himself opposite them. His smile grew even larger as he regarded them. Like he was about to offer them a great deal on a used car. "All right. I understand there was an unfortunate misunderstanding on the floor, Ms. Plotnik. Why don't you tell me all about it?"

Before her mother could say anything, Toni put a hand on her mother's arm and said, "My mother was given those chips. She had no idea they were stolen. I believe I know where more of them are located, but first I want some information about the theft."

The smile dimmed slightly. "And why would you want that?"

Toni could do the fake smile as well as anybody, and she matched Nathan Chisolm in joviality. "I am assisting the police in another matter, but I believe there might be a connection." She was throwing wildly, but hoped very much that the mention of cops would have him more amenable to her deal. She hadn't missed the fact that no one had mentioned turning her mother—or the stolen chips—over to the authorities.

He looked dubious. "May I say you look much too pretty to be a police officer?"

She decided to let the obvious insult to female cops everywhere go. "I'm not a police officer. As I said, I'm assisting the local police in a different matter."

"And you feel there's a connection?"

"I don't know," she answered honestly. "But I think it's possible. What can you tell me about the theft?"

She felt Linda staring at her, but fortunately her mother kept her mouth shut.

He narrowed his eyes as he gazed at her for a moment then, seeming to decide she wasn't going to use the information against him or his employer, said, "You understand this is strictly confidential."

"Of course."

"And my colleague informs me that you are willing to return ten thousand dollars' worth of stolen chips?"

"I am."

He nodded shortly.

"We think it was an inside job."

"Really?"

"Yes. There was no break-in, no burglar waving a gun and an empty sack. But a number of chips went missing."

"When did this happen?"

He paused once more as though debating whether the information was worth ten grand in chips. Finally, he said, "Twelve weeks ago."

"What amount?"

"I'm not at liberty—"

"Mr. Chisolm."

"It was one hundred thousand dollars."

"All in five-hundred-dollar chips?"

"Yes. But our chips are computer coded. The second one of them was played, we could follow the transaction and—" He glanced over at Linda. "Well, you've witnessed exactly what happens."

She looked down through the glass table to their feet, thinking. "If it was an inside job, wouldn't whoever stole them know that they were virtually worthless?"

"You'd think so. Maybe they are selling them at a discount to unsuspecting rub—um, to people who might not understand how tight our security is. We'd like them back so we don't need to inconvenience people like your mother."

She tapped her fingertips lightly against the glass. "Could the chips be tampered with somehow? Could they be modified so they would pass as good?"

He shook his head. "It's never been done." He reached over to his desk and picked up a blue chip that she strongly suspected had recently been played by her mother.

"These chips are made of a very high-tech ceramic. They have a kind of hologram inside. They put them through an ultrasound scanner in the cage and it reads the chips. Catches counterfeits and stolen chips right away. Can't be duplicated or removed. And now, if you have no more questions?"

"Only one. In the last twelve weeks, has anyone else tried to play with the chips?"

"No. Only your mother."

"Thank you." She reached for her bag and pulled out her cell phone, then she pulled the card the Wentworth parking valet had given her from her pocket and dialed the number. "Could I speak to Vernon, please?"

"You are speaking to him."

"Oh, good. Vernon, this is Toni Diamond, you parked my—"

"The rental Prius. I remember you."

Amazing what twenty bucks and a big smile could do. "Excellent. I need you to do something for me. In the glove compartment of my car is a paper lunch sack. Could you bring it up to Mr. Chisolm's office in security?"

He paused at the unusual request, but only for a moment. Then he said, "Yes, ma'am, right away."

"Thank you, Vernon." And she clicked off.

"You left ten thousand dollars in casino chips in your glove compartment?"

She smiled. "I'm sure you'll agree they were safer there than in my handbag where anyone could snatch them."

"Ms. Diamond, you are a remarkable woman."

"Thank you, Mr. Chisolm."

"Could I offer you ladies a beverage while we wait?"

She turned to Linda, who still looked stunned at the turn her day had taken. "Mother?"

"Perhaps a water."

"Ms. Diamond?"

"Water would be good."

He went to a small refrigerator and withdrew three small bottles of water and, from a discreet shelf, brought out three heavy glasses suitable for scotch.

Before he could launch into polite small talk, she threw out a topic she was interested in. "It's a terrible shock about Grant Forstman," she said.

"Hmm?" He unscrewed the cap off his water. "Oh, yeah. Terrible."

"I'm sure, if you were in charge of security at the Double Nugget, such a tragedy could never occur."

"You wouldn't catch me dead at a sleazy place like that," he said. "And if a man has enemies who want him dead badly enough, they'll find a way."

"Did he have a lot of enemies?"

Nathan Chisolm drank water without bothering to pour it into a glass first. "The Double Nugget is one of the last privately owned casinos left in Vegas. Most of the hotels and casinos, like the Wentworth, are owned by movie studios or big hotel chains. Grant Forstman was from the old school. Rumor was he was doing business with people he maybe shouldn't have."

She poured her water into a glass. "You think it was a hit?"

He put down the bottle and it made a clicking sound on the glass tabletop. "I have no idea. Anyway, the police arrested a suspect." He smiled that snake oil salesman smile again. "Now, I could tell you some stories about Vegas in the bad old days that would curl your hair." She listened as Nathan Chisolm reminisced about mob hits and colorful characters. Since he had clearly told her everything useful he was going to, she let him.

A soft knock fell on the door, interrupting a story about Frank Sinatra that might even have been true. "Come in."

The parking attendant appeared holding the paper sack.

"Thank you, Vernon," Toni said, rising. She took the sack and passed it to the head of security. "My mother and I will ride down with you, Vernon, if you don't mind. We'll get our car now."

"Certainly, ma'am."

Chisolm eyeballed the chips inside the bag then reached inside and rapidly counted them. He nodded briefly then rose as though he'd been giving the two women a VIP tour instead of holding her mother against her will.

"Very nice to meet you, ladies," he said, shaking each of their hands as they left.

"Phew," Linda gasped as they hit the elevator. Toni squeezed her mother's shoulder, warning her to keep her mouth shut.

"We just need to make a stop at the ice cream shop and pick up my daughter," she said to Vernon. "We'll meet you at the front entrance."

"I'll have your car all ready for you."

Tiffany was sitting in front of an old-fashioned sundae glass, empty but for some smears of chocolate sauce and a haze of vanilla. She had her cell phone out but looked supremely bored.

"Tiffany, I'm so sorry, baby," Linda cried, rushing up and giving her granddaughter a hug.

"Grandma. You're okay."

"Of course, I'm okay. Your mom bailed me out of casino jail."

"Oh, good. I was getting worried. I almost called Luke."

"You're a smart girl, like your mom," Linda said.

Mother and daughter glanced at each other. "Thanks," they said in unison.

"That sundae looks so good," Linda said.

"Do you want one?"

"Desperately. But not here."

So the three of them left and Toni drove them to the outlet mall, where they should have gone in the first place. They shopped for a happy couple of hours, getting their feet back under them. Then she treated them all to dinner, followed by hot fudge sundaes.

As they sat around the table, Linda said, "I don't understand why Dwayne had stolen poker chips in his bedroom."

"Me, neither." And even more shocking, he'd told Tiffany to go out and use them. What kind of a father got their own daughter to attempt to gamble with stolen casino chips?

She didn't say this aloud, of course, but from the look on

her daughter's face, her thoughts were traveling along a similar path.

"He didn't know they were stolen," Toni said suddenly.

"What are you talking about?" Linda snapped. "He had stolen chips in his bedroom. How could he not know?"

"I can't answer that, but I don't believe for one second that Dwayne would knowingly let Tiffany get caught passing stolen chips."

"I don't think so, either," said Tiffany, sounding relieved and a lot happier.

Toni didn't bother explaining that she didn't believe it because Dwayne was such a great father, but because, as dumb as he was, even he must know that if his daughter got busted, Diamonds to Diamonds, the trail would lead right back to him.

CHAPTER 14

Adornment is never anything but a reflection of the self.

— COCO CHANEL

*L*oretta Forstman looked like a classic grieving widow if you counted only that she was wearing all black.

All black workout wear.

Toni had followed her instructions for getting to the private penthouse suite in the hotel portion of the Double Nugget. The country and western theme made it to the bank of elevators but, following instructions, she found the private elevator that led only to the owners' suite and here the ambiance changed immediately. She stepped into the elevator and saw there were two buttons and a discreet phone. The upper one said 2. That's what she'd been told to press. The lower button said 1. She pushed that one first. Nothing happened.

She pushed 2. Nothing happened.

She picked up the phone and pushed the 2. It rang like a phone and a breathless sounding Loretta answered. "Oh, right, Toni," she said after Toni identified herself. "Come on up."

"Thanks."

Toni pushed the 1 on the phone. The phone rang six times and then cut out.

She pushed the elevator button for 1. Nothing.

She pushed the elevator button for 2. The doors closed so quietly that if she'd had her eyes shut, she wouldn't have noticed. Then the elevator rose as though angels lifted her on their wings.

She arrived at her destination and the doors opened onto a marble foyer. One door faced her. Forstman had the entire penthouse floor. She walked out and rang the doorbell.

The door opened to a glowing Loretta in all black workout wear. She wore a black halter top that plunged low over her showgirl breasts and figure-hugging, black stretch capris. Her hair was tied back from her pink-cheeked face and she was panting. "Hi, Toni. Come on in. I was finishing my workout."

As Toni walked in she was aware of two things at once. The owner's apartment was stunning. Everything screamed expensive, top-of-the-line, from the white leather furniture to the crystal lamps, the plush rugs, and the art on the walls. Toni was no art expert, but she walked forward to a piece that took up the better part of one wall and showed a swimming pool. It was all blues and greens and choppy waves churned up by a swimmer. Something about the style was familiar. "What a lovely piece," she said.

"Thanks. It's a Hockney. David's very collectible." Loretta

dropped the name the way you'd say, 'Oh, thanks. When George Clooney came for dinner, he loved my way with Brussels sprouts.'"

No wonder it had seemed familiar. Tiff had done an essay about Hockney's work and become an enthusiastic fan. Toni suspected you had to be very rich to hang one of the originals on your living room wall.

The second thing Toni was aware of was that she wasn't the only visitor. Sounds of another human being emanated from a closed door off the main room. "Did I catch you at a bad time?" she asked, glancing toward the door.

"No. That's Eric, my personal trainer. Eric?" she called. "Come meet Toni."

Eric walked out, all six and a half feet of gorgeous. She blinked. He looked like a Viking god. When he stepped forward to shake her hand she could see that the blond in his hair had some help from the cosmetics gods, but the raw material they had to work with was beyond compare.

"It's nice to meet you, Toni," he said in lightly accented English.

"You even sound like a Viking," she said, speaking without thinking. Those blue, blue eyes and the wicked chin dimple made her foolish.

When he smiled, she wondered if he and Nathan Chisolm got their teeth whitened at the same place. But she wasn't one to quibble. If he wanted to improve on perfection, she wasn't the woman to stop him.

"I am Danish," he said, not embarrassed at all by her comment.

"He's my personal trainer," Loretta repeated.

"If you were my personal trainer, I'd work out every single day."

Loretta laughed. "I do." She stretched her arms over her head, and Toni was able to tear her gaze away from Eric the Viking long enough to see the tone in the woman's arms.

Loretta walked up to Eric and kissed him lightly on the cheek. "Same time tomorrow?"

"Yeah, sure." He sent Toni one more dazzling smile and said, "Nice to meet you. See you tomorrow, Loretta," and he was gone.

"Oh, be still my heart," Toni said.

Loretta laughed, a low, throaty, sexy sound. "I know. Nice eye candy. He's also a very good trainer. If you're in the market."

"In Texas, I would be."

"So, you're heading back soon?"

"Yep, pretty soon. I've got to get my daughter back to school."

"Of course. It's too bad all this trouble had to happen while she was visiting, poor kid."

"You said it."

Toni gestured to the large cosmetics case she was carrying. "Where would you like to do the makeover?"

"Oh, I don't know. I hadn't thought about it." Loretta glanced around the apartment. "What do you suggest?"

"Maybe that nice leather armchair over there? There's a good light I can use and I'll drape the chair to make sure it stays clean."

"Sounds perfect."

~

Toni had always found that a woman being pampered, smoothing wonderful creams onto her face and neck and having her feet up and nothing to focus on for the next sixty minutes but her appearance, tended to treat the makeover chair like a confession booth or a therapist's couch.

Lady Bianca had strict rules laid down for her beauty consultants. They were to teach clients how to apply the creams and lotions, never to apply the creams themselves. So, she pulled out the battery operated makeup mirror, flipping the switch so it lit up, and kept her voice soothing as she described the exfoliating cream Loretta was smoothing into her skin. "It's made from a special seaweed you can only get off the coast of Japan. It's not at all drying, simply polishes the skin surface."

"Feels good," the woman murmured.

"You have such nice skin," she said.

"I'm lucky that way."

Toni could see Loretta's facial muscles relax under the pampering creams. "I can tell you've looked after yourself."

"My face and body were my meal ticket. I've known that since I was fourteen years old and first got scouted by a modeling agency in Phoenix."

Toni nodded. "You're so beautiful. I'm not surprised. Did you model long?"

A bitter laugh was her answer. "Do you have any idea how many pretty girls there are in the world? And how few ever make it in the modeling world? I had a couple of years where I did some runway work and did some underwear modeling for department stores. I was even featured on a national campaign once. But I never had that mysterious thing that sets some girls apart."

She sighed with pleasure when they moved on to a deep moisturizing cream. She smoothed the cream in an upward motion onto her face as Toni directed, and stroked down her neck. "I was dancing to stay in shape, and I ended up in dance class with a girl who worked in Vegas. She said the money was good and there were a lot of rich guys here." She shrugged her toned shoulders. "I thought, what the hell? And came out."

"And she was right?"

"On both counts." She smiled. Her eyes were on her own reflection so Toni had a chance to really look at the woman, naked and vulnerable. "I was an honest-to-God Vegas show-girl when I met Grant. Of course, he was married, but he liked to watch me dance, and he liked to spend money on me. I was over thirty. I knew the clock was ticking and my time to get myself settled was running out."

There was something about Loretta's brutal honesty that Toni had to admire. "I bet you were stunning."

"Once he had me working at the Nugget, he'd sneak me up to his office between shows. It was our special place." She sighed in memory. "Those were good days."

"And after you were married? Did you still visit him in his office?"

"Not so much. It wasn't as much fun when it was legal, if you know what I mean." Then she shifted. "Grant didn't think so either, obviously."

"Obviously? You mean...?"

"Hey, we're both women who've been screwed over by men. We know the score. He found a younger model."

"Your husband was having an affair?"

The plump lips thinned. "He'd come home smelling like perfume and it wasn't mine."

"Any idea who she was?"

"No." Toni saw the muscles of Loretta Forstman's face clench briefly. The involuntary tightening was as efficient as a polygraph at telling Toni that Loretta was lying. She knew perfectly well who her husband had been seeing.

As they finished the skincare regime and moved on to the cosmetics application, Toni adapted to her client. A makeover was about psychology as well as sales. How does this client see herself in the world? When you can paint them the way they see themselves in their dreams, you've made a big sale.

Loretta had already told Toni what she wanted. She wanted to look like the fresh young Vegas showgirl who'd attracted the high roller, the whale. Toni pulled out her most dramatic palette, showed Loretta how to go a little heavier than normal, emphasizing the cat-like eyes and the Marilyn Monroe mouth.

When she was done, Loretta laughed in delight. "I could go on stage right now."

"Too much?"

She shook her head, turning this way and that to admire her reflection. "Perfect. I'm seeing Grant's lawyer later. I like the war paint." She gave Toni back the mirror. "You did a great job. I'll buy everything you demonstrated. I need to treat myself after what I've been through."

"I so agree," Toni said. "You know, I think you could be a wonderful addition to our team. Would you consider becoming a Lady Bianca rep yourself? I can tell you running your own independent cosmetics business can be very lucrative."

Loretta blinked her stiffened lashes. "You think I need a job?"

Toni waved her hands delicately. "I have no idea how you were left, obviously, but if you want to earn a little extra money or a lot of money, Lady Bianca is—"

A husky laugh cut her off. "Honey, I will never have to work again." She leaned forward, smiling the smile that must have captivated Grant Forstman. "Thanks to a wonderful little thing called life insurance."

CHAPTER 15

False face must hide what the dark heart doth know.

— WILLIAM SHAKESPEARE

ife insurance, thought Toni as she headed back down the private elevator. Money. A cheating husband. A motive within a motive.

And there was the very interesting extra stop on the private elevator ride that had her extremely curious. Dollars to donuts that elevator stopped at Grant's private office and his home. If she was right, this was the biggest break yet in her efforts to free her ex-husband of a murder charge.

What if the video cameras hadn't caught the murderer going into the office because the killer hadn't entered in the same way Dwayne did, through the front door? What if there was a private entrance to Forstman's office from his own elevator? One he kept quiet about except to a select group.

The best way to find out was to go back to Grant Forstman's office and see if anyone felt like gossiping.

She tried again to stop at that mysterious stop numbered one, but again the efficient elevator swooped her all the way down to the main floor and deposited her like King Kong putting Faye Wray gently on the ground.

She had to get into Forstman's office and sniff out what she could about that elevator. She stood still for a moment and then, making up her mind on a plan of action, headed for one of the casino level washrooms. Once inside, she made full use of the cosmetics in her case, adding drama and using sexier colors than she'd normally use for daytime. She painted her lips a deep plum, making them seem larger with the skillful use of a lip pencil and gloss. Her hair hung in soft curls, so she wet her fingers at the bathroom sink and pushed them through her thick hair, giving her a sultry mane. Finally, she removed her jacket and unbuttoned her blouse by another button.

Toni was well-endowed by nature, and though she didn't usually advertise her assets, it seemed this might be an occasion when it was worth her while to do so. Not wanting to drag her professional cosmetics case with her, she dashed to the show lounge. As she'd hoped, Sunny and the Three Chers were already there. Without Dwayne, they were having to reshuffle their line-up.

When she arrived, a meeting was in progress on stage. She recognized everyone but one man, a guy with a guitar who had presumably been hauled in to replace her incarcerated ex. The backup entertainers were sitting at scattered tables. She wanted to catch Sunny's eye and see if she could leave her case in his dressing room, but he was in intense conversation with the new guy.

She didn't want to hike her bag all the way down to her car. Could she simply leave it here?

She checked out the tables. A full-figured blond sat alone at one. She kept rubbing a diamond ring and turning it around on her finger. Toni vaguely remembered her as a backup singer in the Salute to Broadway act. She walked over and leaned over the table, making eye contact with the sad-looking woman. "Don't tell me, he promised you a diamond and it turned out to be a cubic zirconia?"

Big blue eyes blinked at her. "No," the showgirl said, her eyes welling with sudden tears. "He died."

"Oh, I'm so sorry." And inside she said, *Oh, I can't believe my luck*. If this woman wasn't Forstman's latest mistress, then her name wasn't Toni Diamond. "I'm Toni Plotnik," she said. "I have some makeup for Sunny and the Three Chers. Is it okay if I leave it in their dressing room?"

"Sure. I guess."

"Could you show me where it is?"

"Yeah. Sure."

When the woman rose, Toni saw that she was tall. Tall, blond, statuesque. Grant Forstman certainly was consistent. He was like a man who bought a new car every five years but always chose the same make and model. Only the year was newer.

They headed down a dark corridor to the dressing rooms. "This one's theirs," the young woman said.

On impulse, Toni touched her arm. "I'm so sorry for your loss."

"It's so hard," she whispered. "We were going to get married."

"Really?" She couldn't stop her surprise. Did the man actually marry them all or only promise to?

"This is my engagement ring. Of course I couldn't wear it on the proper finger until he got divorced." She sniffed. "Now, this is all I'll ever have of him."

They were standing in a narrow hallway and she opened the dressing room door and saw it was empty. Two long counters with brightly-lit mirrors took up the bulk of the room. A rack on the third wall bulged with the glittery costumes. Wigs and shoes were arranged on shelves. "Where do you think I should leave the makeup case?" she asked.

As she'd hoped, Forstman's last girlfriend stepped into the room with her, gazing vaguely around. "I guess you could leave it on the floor, underneath the makeup stations."

"Good idea." She stowed her case and then turned before the other woman could leave. "And you never got to say a proper good-bye?"

Once more she turned the ring around on her finger. "No."

"When was the last time you saw Grant?" She had her fingers mentally crossed that she'd guessed right and was rewarded when the girl teared up again.

"The day he, you know."

"The same day he was killed?"

She nodded. "We didn't have as much fun as usual. He was preoccupied about something. But at least I got to spend one more afternoon with the man I loved." She sniffled again.

"Afternoon?"

"Sure. We always met in the afternoon. I work at night and he always liked to keep an eye on the casino when it was busy. Sometimes he'd come in and catch the show."

"Isn't that elevator amazing?" she said, just two girls gossiping about stuff.

Those blue eyes opened wide and she checked Toni out, looking her up and down. "You've been in the elevator?"

"Only up to the apartment," she hastily assured her new friend. "I never even met Mr. Forstman. I had to deliver something to his apartment once."

"Oh. Oh, yeah. The elevator's something."

As they left the dressing room, she shut the door behind them. "I don't even know your name."

"Oh, right. My name is Goldie."

She touched the woman's shoulder. "I really am sorry, Goldie," she said.

SHE FOUND her way once more to the administration level and down the hall toward Grant Forstman's office. It was Tuesday and the place was buzzing with staff. A certain quiver of anxiety hung in the air. She imagined people were wondering about the future of the casino and of their livelihood.

As she trod purposefully down the corridor, she wondered herself what would happen to the Double Nugget.

There was no cop standing guard outside the dead casino owner's office today. Instead, a woman with softly curling gray hair and a determined face sat in one of the offices that faced the hallway. It was the one closest to Forstman's so she had to assume the woman was an executive assistant of some kind. She emerged from her office before Toni could so much as make a grab for the handle on the closed door of Forstman's office.

"May I help you?"

"Yes. Well. I hope so." She did her best to channel the young woman who claimed to be engaged to the oft-married Mr. Forstman. She made her voice a little softer, spoke a little slower. "I think I dropped an earring in Mr. Forstman's office." She opened her hand to show one of the diamond earrings she'd hastily taken off on her way up here. Its mate sat zipped into her change purse.

Toni could see the older woman controlling her eyeballs from rolling with contempt but it wasn't easy. One of them was twitching. "When was this?"

She tried to look as dumb as this woman obviously believed her to be. "About a week ago?"

"And yet I've never seen you before. I see everyone who goes in and out of Mr. Forstman's office."

Toni took a breath designed to show off her impressive cleavage. "He let me up in his private elevator."

The woman's gaze was so piercing she felt holes ripping in her skin. Soon her blood and organs would spill out. Finally, she said, "The cleaners come in every night. If they'd found jewelry, they'd have turned it in. I haven't seen anything."

She tried to look coy and embarrassed. "I think the earring might have fallen down the back of the leather couch when Mr. Forstman and me were, um, meeting."

"Uh, huh? Why don't you give me your name and phone number? I'll take a look for you."

"Please, it will only take five minutes. Could I just run in there and look? The earrings were a gift." She did her best to look teary and forlorn. "My last gift from Grant."

She could see the denial forming when suddenly a voice yelled, "Myrna, the guys are here about the buyout. Can you come down here?"

"Leave your information on my desk," the woman snapped and then ran down the hall and disappeared into one of the doors further down.

And before you could say "No Trespassing," Toni was easing open the door to Grant Forstman's office and slipping inside.

She closed the door softly behind her then took a moment to simply stand still and take in all her impressions. She could still smell cigar smoke but it was growing fainter. The chemical smells deposited by the CSI team were sharper, newer scents, and there was the low note of death hanging like the aroma of rot.

She wasn't like one of those psychics on TV who could tell you what happened by communing with spirits or anything, but she found, if she stood very still and let herself take a moment that she could take in an atmosphere. In this case, what she felt was a profound stillness. It was like being closed inside an airless cellar or something. Then she realized there was no window in the office. All the opulence of expensive furniture and décor and yet no window to let in fresh air or light or the outside world.

If Grant Forstman had shuttled between his home, his office and his casino, she wondered if he ever went outside.

She could not see an elevator door, but she was certain it was here. She ran her fingers along the wall beside the door and felt smooth drywall. The wall beside it housed the couch and was similarly elevator free. Behind the desk was wooden paneling that extended to two walls. It was dark, rich, expensive and seamed. How would you know if one of the seams was the opening for an elevator?

She didn't know how much time she had but felt it wouldn't be long. When Myrna didn't find a name and address on her desk, Toni had a gut feeling she'd be in here making sure the shrine of her dead employer remained undisturbed.

The third wall contained the safe. It was behind the desk but not hidden in any way. It looked heavy and mean as though daring anyone to try to break in. Of course, she knew one man who'd been foolish enough to do exactly that.

She headed for the fourth wall. It featured the same wooden paneling. Did one of the seams appear slightly darker? Yes, she thought it did. Okay, if this was the elevator, where was the call button? She scooted over to the desk and ran her hands over all the surfaces. Nothing.

She began scanning the walls looking for irregularities, anything sticking out. She found it in a fake knot. So cleverly disguised she'd have missed it had she not been certain it was there. When she pushed that button there was no sound, but in ten seconds the door opened.

She stepped inside the elevator and pressed 2. Nothing happened. So you must need some kind of code. She imagined that Grant Forstman had been very careful when he had this elevator designed. He didn't want his women running into each other. And a man who didn't have the most savory of associates would always want a back door. A place to disappear from if he needed to escape.

She heard voices outside the door. She was reaching for

the panel when the office door opened and Myrna stood there with her eyes bugging out. Before she could say a word, Toni flashed the earring along with her biggest smile. "Found it." At the same moment, Myrna turned her head and yelled, "Milo!"

When she pushed the button for lobby, the elevator doors closed and she slid down without a hitch.

As she headed out of the elevator door she remembered what her mother had said about the abundance of security cameras and glanced around her.

"Bingo."

And then she figured she'd better move fast because she had a feeling that Milo was going to be looking for her.

CHAPTER 16

There must be quite a few things that a hot bath won't cure, but I don't know many of them.

— SYLVIA PLATH

Toni sped out of the casino as fast as if, oh, say a gorilla who hurt people for a living was after her.

She was breathless when she hit the street. Of course, this being the Double Nugget and not the Wentworth, there were no cabs or plush limos lining the entrance courtyard. There was no lovely Vernon dressed like a Janeite's wet dream to leap into action and call up a carriage.

What she spotted, after a minute of scanning the streets, was an actual carriage. A horse-drawn buggy that no doubt hauled brides and grooms back and forth to the many chapels. However, it was the only transport and the horse was plodding so slowly, its head down and hay on its mind, that she sprinted across the street and leapt into the passenger seat before the driver even saw her coming.

"Hey," he said in surprise, turning. "Whatcha doin'?"

He sounded like Brooklyn and like he might pull over and dump her off unceremoniously at the curb. "I was waving," she panted, "but you didn't see me." While she was wheezing, she dug out her wallet and pulled out a hundred-dollar bill. She pushed it at the guy. "Please, it's always been my dream to ride in a horse-drawn carriage."

"Lyin' down?"

He turned to regard her. She had assumed the fetal position, hoping Milo might not notice her if she made herself very small.

But that wasn't going to work if the driver turned to stare at her and dropped the reins.

"Please," she said, figuring some version of the truth was her best bet at getting the guy's cooperation. "I need to get out of here."

He glanced up and down the street, then turned back and said something to the horse. Whatever it was, the horse picked up the pace. Her driver didn't turn again, but said, as though he were talking to his horse, but loud enough that she could hear, "Would the guy looking for you be Eastern European? About two hundred fifty pounds, wearing a dark suit and sweating?"

"Yeah."

"Okay. Keep your head down. I haven't lost a passenger yet." And with those fateful words, he clicked his tongue and the horse broke into a trot. Her ride was far from comfortable but a hell of a lot better, she suspected, than whatever Milo would have done to her.

About ten minutes later, he said, "You can sit up now. Guy's long gone."

"Thanks," she said, sitting up. She tried to right the mess of her hair, but in a jolting carriage she suspected she was making things worse.

"Where do I let you off?"

She'd been wondering that herself. They passed a bridal chapel and a wedding dress store and a stationery store that promised *invitations, keepsakes, albums and more.* "Could you pull over here?"

"Sure thing." He pulled over to the side of the road and she jumped out.

"Thank you," she said.

"Stay out of trouble." And with a wave, he was gone with a faint clip clop of hooves.

She smoothed down her skirt, buttoned the top of her blouse and slipped her jacket back on. Then she walked into the Hearts Aflame Stationery Store.

"Hi," she said to the thin, older man wearing a button-up sweater and a Hitler mustache. "Do you do business cards?"

"Could do. Mostly we print wedding stuff. But you can have anything you want."

She purchased the smallest quantity of business cards the guy would sell her. One hundred. She designed the business cards right on a computer in the store. Not wanting anyone to clue in that she shared a name with the guy currently charged with Forstman's murder, she typed Toni Plotnik, Private Investigator, and she added her cell phone number. She toyed with adding a cute logo, like a deerstalker cap and a little magnifying glass, but she decided a simple card would look more professional and also be easier to forget about than something eye-catching.

She called a cab from the stationery store and headed

back to the hotel, deciding to leave her car where it was at the Double Nugget. She'd retrieve it later.

She returned to the hotel, found her mother and daughter sprawled happily in front of the TV watching a movie.

"How'd you make out?" Linda asked her.

For a second she wondered how on earth her mother had divined that she'd been snooping then she realized she was referring to the makeover. How long ago that seemed now. And her makeup case was still in the dressing room. She'd have to remember to retrieve it.

"The makeover was fabulous. She bought everything I put on her face. Everything!"

"Hah!" Her mother was so delighted she jumped up and high-fived her daughter.

Tiffany said, "If my husband just got killed, I wouldn't rush out and buy a bunch of makeup. That is so cold."

She was glad she hadn't mentioned Eric, the Viking god. She smiled at her daughter. "We all grieve in different ways, honey. Sitting around crying all day won't bring her husband back."

In fact, Toni had tried that with Dwayne, who wasn't even dead, and it certainly hadn't brought him back.

"But I understand what you're saying." She stretched her arms over her head. "I'm going to have a bath and then how about we go out for dinner? I missed lunch and I'm starving." After they'd both agreed, she said, "Oh, and I booked a couple of tickets to Cirque du Soleil. As good as the Double Nugget's show is, it would be nice for you two to see some of the other Vegas offerings."

"Two of us? Aren't you coming?" her daughter wanted to know.

"I have to work tonight. But I'll meet you after the show and maybe you and me can get pizza or something while we let grandma hit the slot machines. What do you think?"

Linda shuddered. "I am never going near a casino again."

"You gotta get back on the horse that threw you, Mom."

Linda was pretty easy to convince. "But this time I'll use my own money."

Toni used one of the French mud relaxation masks, grabbed a large glass of water and retreated to the tub. She'd always found that a hot bath was not only relaxing but also a good place to think.

While the facial mask rejuvenated her complexion, and the water rehydrated her, she lay back in the tub and let the facts she knew, the impressions she'd gained, roll around like the little balls on the roulette tables.

She felt as though her results were as random.

One thing she was certain of, though. That elevator was the missing piece of the puzzle.

She got out of the bath with renewed determination. She redid her makeup, going with a light evening look. Then she did her hair in a completely different style using some of her mother's clip-in hair extensions. She wore black slacks, a black stretchy top, with just a little glitter woven through the fabric, and heels. She looked as different from the woman who had entered Forstman's office as it was possible for her to look.

The Cirque du Soleil show was in one of the big hotels near theirs, so she was able to walk her mom and daughter over without anyone noticing she didn't have her car. They found an Italian restaurant and pigged out on pasta and bread and salad. Then she walked the other two women to the entrance to the Cirque Theater and left them in the store browsing everything from CDs to Christmas ornaments. They promised to meet up after the show, and she was happy to see that her daughter was looking brighter and happier. Also, without any discussion, they seemed to assume Tiffany would be spending the night with them in the hotel.

Tiffany was learning the hard way that her father was a charmer, but not someone you could count on.

Before grabbing a cab back to the Double Nugget, she found a relatively quiet spot in a marble alcove near a bar that hadn't opened yet and called Luke.

"Marciano." It wasn't even a bark, more a growl, so she knew Luke was tired. It was early evening on a weekday when she wasn't in town, so she suspected he'd hit the gym on his way home, probably picked up something easy for dinner.

She didn't waste time. "How do I get to see footage from the security cameras at the Double Nugget?"

"The police already have the footage, Toni. That's how they caught your ex-husband coming out of Grant Forstman's office around the time of the murder."

"Well, guess what? There's a secret elevator to his office."

She heard the sound of a beer can opening. "A secret elevator?" He did not sound convinced.

"Yep. I don't think the police here even know about it. They arrested Dwayne faster 'n spit dries in the desert. Nobody ever did a proper investigation."

"Your Texas country accent is getting stronger. You must be pissed."

"I am." She tried to modulate her voice. Shorten the

vowel sounds. "I do not love Dwayne Diamond even a little bit, but I don't want to see an innocent man punished. No, that's not right. I don't want to see a cheat, a liar, and a thief punished for murder. He should be punished for those other things, though." Fair was fair. "Luke, they have the death penalty in Nevada. He was supposed to get a defense investigator but the guy's tied up for a month."

"Okay, let's back up a sec here. Are you absolutely positive that there is a second entrance to that office?" In spite of himself he was sounding interested. And who could blame him? It was pretty fine investigating on her part.

"I rode the elevator myself. I got into it in Grant Forstman's office and I rode it down to the lobby. It's tucked out of sight of the main bank of elevators but it's there all right. It's the same elevator that goes to his apartment upstairs. There are only two stops. And there's a security camera outside the elevator. I want to see that footage."

There was a metallic thud on the other end of the line that sounded like a metal beer can being banged down on a surface. She held the phone away from her ear.

"What the hell were you doing in Grant Forstman's office?" he exploded. "That is a crime scene and you could end up being arrested as an accessory to murder faster 'n spit dries in the desert."

"I had to do something," she argued, but that sounded kind of lame. In truth, she'd been so caught up in proving the existence of that secret ride that she hadn't thought through the possible consequences.

Not that that would have stopped her, obviously, but she might have been more circumspect about telling Luke how she knew about the elevator.

"You are pushy and put your nose where it has no business," he ranted.

"Well, somebody has to find the real killer."

"There's a process to police work, Toni. There's logic and steps—"

"Can't you even give me a little credit for figuring this out? I'm a private investigator. I'm investigating privately."

She heard him swallow some of his beer. Then after a moment, he said, "First, in Nevada, a private investigator needs a license. If you're caught acting like a PI without one, you could get slapped with a misdemeanor, probation, even jail time."

"Oh. I didn't know that." Shoot. She was going to have to be a lot more careful.

"Second, you are the chief suspect's ex-wife." She could hear his frustration. "I wish you were here right now eating Thai. I'd know you were safe. I could keep an eye on you. Find something better to occupy your time than getting involved in a police investigation where you could get yourself into serious trouble."

Okay, he was no sweet talker, but she knew he was telling her he worried about her. "So that's what you're having. Thai. And you went to the gym after work, right?"

"Yeah."

She sighed. Knew his hair would be damp and he'd be freshly shaved. He always used the steam room and shaved after his gym workout. Well, maybe he didn't bother shaving if he wasn't going to be seeing her. How would she know? "I wish I was there, too."

"I can pass on your finding to the cops down there."

163

She knew a little bit about how the policing system worked. Enough to say, "Will they let me see the footage?"

"Probably not." Which seemed completely unfair since she'd discovered the elevator.

She didn't tell Luke about the hundred business cards in her purse. She should have put something else on the cards. Background Researcher, maybe. Something that wouldn't get her slapped in jail along with her ex-husband. Well, she didn't have time to worry about that now. Her plan was to try to sweet talk somebody in security into letting her view the tapes, but after Luke's last outburst she decided to keep that part of her plan to herself.

She felt in her bones that this was the breakthrough they needed. "The existence of that elevator fits in with Dwayne saying he heard Grant pick up his phone and say, 'Hey, baby.' He was letting some woman up in the elevator."

"Some woman who planned to shoot him?"

"Okay, it's not a perfect theory. I'm still working on it."

Based on her conversation with Luke, she wasn't going to get to that surveillance footage through official channels. It was great that Luke was going to suggest to the LVPD that they check out the cameras near that private elevator, but she was the one who'd made the breakthrough. She should be the one to see the footage.

Besides, she wanted to know who'd killed Grant Forstman. The mistress? The wife? Some as yet unidentified person he called baby?

She hoped she'd know very soon.

The cab dropped her off and she headed into the Double Nugget.

Having experienced the Wentworth Casino security, the Double Nugget's setup fell a little short of her expectations.

She was hoping that both Myrna and Milo would have gone home for the day. She wasn't so sure about Milo, but then he'd never seen her. Of course, she'd been so busy checking for surveillance cameras when she left that elevator that she'd stared right into the cameras. Had he viewed that footage? Hopefully, she'd changed her appearance enough that he wouldn't recognize her even if he had seen her on camera. And she'd definitely be trying to stay out of his way.

The security department was not as high tech as the Wentworth. Also, with the owner dead, she sensed that things in general were a little lax. She knew from Brent that there was a general manager as well as plenty of middle managers, but somehow without Grant Forstman's looming presence, she felt that maybe things were a little looser. She hoped so.

She walked through the casino and picked out the security people. She deliberately chose a young guy who was so hopelessly in love with a blackjack dealer that he was practically leaving drool marks on her white blouse.

"Excuse me," she said to him.

"Yeah?" He was so not interested in helping her. Perfect.

"I need to find the surveillance room."

"The what?"

She had no idea what it was called. "The place where they store the footage from the security cameras."

He might be obsessed with a girl but he wasn't completely stupid. He narrowed his eyes, looked her up and down. "What do you want security footage for?"

She drew out one of her new cards and showed it to him. "I'm here on behalf of a client."

As she'd hoped, he stared at the card but didn't take it. Phew.

She sweet talked her way into a room where banks of TVs showed various hallways and portions of the lobbies.

The man in charge of this wealth of footage seemed delighted to have company. He barely glanced at her business card and once more, she slipped it back into her bag. "Sure. Come in. Make yourself at home." He was a chubby man in his early forties. Balding and bored. "I'm Buddy Olafson."

"Toni Plotnik." She shook his hand. Like him, it was chubby, a little soft.

She explained what she was looking for. "The footage from the evening of May tenth from the cameras outside Mr. Forstman's private elevator."

"You came to the right place. As you can see, I don't do the casino surveillance; that's a whole nother division. I keep an eye on the hotel and the lobbies." He sounded almost defensive that he got the boring part of the job.

"I'm sure a lot goes on," she said, trying to cheer him up.

He chuckled. "You got that right." He shook his head. "I've seen people have fights, break up, get engaged, puke, and the number of people who have sex in public places, well—" He shook his head.

"I can't imagine." Having sex in the lobby of the Double Nugget? She seriously couldn't imagine that even Eric the gorgeous Viking could tempt her. Okay, for Eric the gorgeous Viking, she might make an exception.

Buddy cracked his knuckles. "May the tenth? That's the night Mr. Forstman died."

"Yes. It is."

"How come you want to see it? The cops never asked for that. They only asked about the cameras outside his office."

"I'm assisting the police in their inquiries," she said. It was true in a way. Proving they had the wrong guy would definitely assist the police.

He accepted her story. "Okay. You can look but I can't let you take anything away with you. Not without a warrant."

"I only want to look at the footage. But the police will probably come for it fairly soon." Unless the footage showed no action at all outside Mr. Forstman's private elevator, in which case her new discovery was about as valuable as one of Dwayne's stolen casino chips.

"Okay. So long as there's a warrant."

He hummed while he worked, cracking his knuckles every few minutes as though that was part of the process. Eventually, he said. "Okay. There are three cameras that watch the area around Mr. and Mrs. Forstman's private elevator."

He cued up the footage. "You can see the time, right there, in the corner. It's date stamped as well."

"Great. Thank you."

He pulled over a chair on wheels for her and sat back in his own. They settled side by side to watch the TV as though it was a movie and they were on a date. "Bet you wish we had popcorn," her chubby host joked.

"Yes." *No.*

She'd asked him to start reviewing at ten o'clock that evening to be on the safe side.

He put the video on fast mo and nothing happened. She watched the carpet and the walls from three different cameras. At ten thirty-five a figure appeared and Toni felt her pulse quicken. He slowed the tape to normal speed. The woman striding forward as though getting ready to do a high kick was Loretta Forstman. She wore a figure-hugging black dress that struck envy into Toni's heart, her diamonds, and a scowl. Toni watched as she entered the range of the first of the three cameras, then was picked up by camera two and finally the third, right outside the elevator doors. She entered the elevator and, where Toni had called up, she entered a code.

Toni made a note of the time in her notebook. She also jotted down a question. Could anyone watching this footage be able to figure out the code? She'd have to ask Luke. Perhaps someone like her new friend Buddy, with a lot of time on his hands, could watch over and over again as she punched in that code until he figured out the number sequence.

More time lapsed. A cleaner with a cart trundled through. Picked up by camera one, then two, and then back again. The cleaner never made it to camera three because he didn't bother going all the way to the end of the corridor. Sloppy.

Nothing happened. The minutes crept by.

It was eleven. Eleven-thirty. Coming up to midnight. She felt a tension in her belly. Her entire theory was based on Dwayne thinking he'd heard Forstman on the phone saying, "Hey, baby."

Eleven fifty-six. Fifty-seven. A figure came into view. Loretta again? The woman was tall, with the same long, blond hair. She had her head down and she was wearing a different outfit than Loretta had worn earlier. She wore dark pants, a loose jacket that looked like silk. High heels. "Come on, look up," Toni ordered silently.

Either the woman knew about the cameras and didn't want her face to show, or she was contemplating the pattern in the flooring, or thinking deep thoughts. She entered the range of camera two and she was still looking down.

Camera three caught her again. Now she pushed the button and entered the elevator. Yes! She picked up the phone. Didn't enter a code, but pushed a button as Toni had done when she was first let up to the Forstman's apartment.

Toni could picture the scenario. Dwayne leaving Forstman's office, maybe pausing to get rid of the cigar so he'd heard not only the phone ringing, but Grant Forstman answering it, saying, "Hey, baby."

The woman's back was to the camera so Toni had no idea what she said but pretty clearly, Grant Forstman had replied with some version of, "Come on up."

And then the elevator doors closed.

Toni pictured the woman riding the elevator up to his office. He'd expected a roll on the casting couch with the woman he'd promised would be Mrs. Forstman the Fourth. What he'd received was a couple of bullets in the chest.

"Yes!" she cried. "That's it." She turned to pat Buddy on his ample shoulder. "Thank you."

Buddy didn't seem as excited by her finding. "This is important? Miss, I don't mean no disrespect, but Mr. Forstman was my boss. I don't want it getting out that he was cheating on Mrs. Forstman."

"Of course not. The police need to see who used the elevator the night of Mr. Forstman's death. You know police work. It's all dotting the i's and crossing the t's."

She asked him to play the last couple of minutes back again, but she couldn't identify the elevator user. She copied down the exact times from the monitor into her notebook.

She rose from her chair and gathered her things. Replacing her notebook and pen in her bag, she thanked Buddy once again.

He cracked his knuckles. "Okay." He sounded disappointed. She wasn't sure if he was sorry about his boss cheating or that she was leaving so soon.

"Are you absolutely certain I can't have a copy of that?" She felt an urgency within her to run it down to the precinct right away.

He shook his head. "Like I said. We have rules and I gotta follow them. You need a warrant."

"Okay. The police will be here very soon. Probably tomorrow. Promise me you'll guard that with your life."

"Nobody gets to that film except over my dead body," he promised her.

CHAPTER 17

Adults are just outdated children.

— DR. SEUSS

*D*wayne might only be out on bail, but he wasn't the kind of person to worry about trivialities. He was free right now and with Dwayne that was good enough. He clearly believed now that Toni had managed to get him out of jail that she'd keep him out.

Tiffany was counting on her too and she was determined to do her best. Especially now that she was certain Dwayne hadn't killed Forstman.

After the way Luke had yelled at her about her visit to the dead man's office, she'd almost by-passed him and gone straight to the LVPD with her discovery of the footage, but she knew the chances weren't huge that they'd drop everything because the ex-wife of their prime suspect thought she'd seen the real murderer on a surveillance camera.

She'd called him right after she collected her car and

headed back to her hotel. He'd threatened some very painful things when she admitted that she'd gone back to the casino and sweet-talked security into letting her see that footage.

Luke might be mad at her, but she knew that he respected her intelligence and her instincts. If he told the local cops to check out surveillance footage, they were more likely to do so.

Even though he'd still been pretty huffy after she'd told him what she'd seen, she could tell he was interested. "The girlfriend, huh? You're sure?"

"No. I'm not a hundred percent positive. She never looked up at the camera, but who would if they were planning to kill someone? Besides, Forstman had to know the killer. He had to let her up. She must be the person who phoned when Dwayne was walking out. How many people would Forstman call 'baby?'"

"According to what I'm hearing, most of the showgirls in Vegas."

That was true, but she liked her theory that his latest girl-friend had found out he wasn't going to marry her or that he was broke or something that made her decide to kill him. "She seemed so sweet. The last person you'd expect to kill anybody." She recalled those tears. They'd seemed real.

"What about Mrs. Forstman? Sounds like she had more to lose."

"I know. And I guess she could have changed clothes, come back down some other way, and then called her husband from the lobby. She'd have to call him. She couldn't access his office from the private elevator without his okay."

"So, she calls up the husband, suggests a nightcap. A quickie on the office couch to bring back happy memories?"

"Something like that, I guess." She felt the frustration of almost but not quite knowing who was on that tape. "I sure wish she'd looked up. The guy in charge of surveillance wouldn't give me a copy of the tape. Make sure the cops get it, okay? This is the evidence that will free Dwayne."

"I'm calling them the second I hang up with you."

"Thanks."

"And Toni?"

"Yeah?"

"You keep your nose clean and let the cops handle this. You hear me? Killers have a reputation of being dangerous."

"I'll be good," she promised.

She shared her story with Linda and only Linda. Her mom looked a little disappointed. "Goldie sounded so sweet. I didn't want it to be her." She let out a sigh.

"I know."

In honor of Dwayne's first night back at the Double Nugget after his recent incarceration, he'd insisted his three angels, as he'd taken to calling them, come watch his show. She'd wondered if her ex would find himself unemployed, seeing as he was accused of murdering the man who'd owned the Double Nugget. But it seemed the Double Nugget didn't hold grudges.

In the Broadway revival number, Toni nudged her mother when Forstman's girlfriend came on. "There's Goldie."

Linda watched for a moment in silence, then turned to Toni. "She's counting her steps. You can see her lips moving. And you're telling me that bimbo murdered Forstman?"

"I saw her on camera."

"That girl doesn't look like she could kill a mosquito if it landed on her arm and was sucking out her blood."

Toni had to agree that the showgirl wouldn't be the first person you'd turn to if you wanted someone killed.

When Sunny and the Three Chers came out, Linda clapped so hard she was in danger of carpal tunnel syndrome. "Don't they look so much better with the new makeup?"

Linda was justifiably proud of the sales she'd made to the female impersonators. Most people wouldn't notice under the stage lights, in glittery costumes and outrageous head-pieces that their makeup was more alluring, but Toni could see it right away. "They look fantastic. You're an artist."

"I have a knack," her mom admitted.

Sunny and the Three Chers were as fun to watch the second time as they had been the first.

Dwayne, not so much. He came to the mic and glanced around the room. "Thank you, ladies and gentlemen, for your warm welcome. I am so happy to be back with you all at the Double Nugget." He paused for dramatic effect and in the pause Toni could hear an already drunk patron loudly ordering a whiskey sour. "When a man's been unfairly incarcerated," Dwayne continued, "he has a lot of time to think."

Linda snorted. "He was in there for three days."

"He gets to know what really matters. I'd like to dedicate this next song to my three angels. My daughter, Tiffany, and my wife, Toni, and the woman I sometimes call Mom."

As he rolled into "You are the Only One for Me," Linda leaned over and said, "And he should hear what I sometimes call him."

When the show ended, all the performers came out for a drink. Dwayne had insisted he was going to buy everybody a drink to celebrate his release from jail. Dwayne had the ability to make a party out of anything and she gave him credit. All the cast and a few of the audience members still hanging around seemed to be having a good time.

Linda sipped on a margarita and watched the waiter make the rounds. "So, who do you figure is paying for this? You or Brent?"

She was under no illusions that Dwayne was picking up the tab. He'd take credit for his generosity and stick somebody else with the bill. "Probably me. Unless he's crazy enough to put a round of drinks on Loretta Forstman's bill."

Linda snorted with laughter. "Knowing Dwayne? I believe he would be dumb enough to charge his drinks to the wife of the man he's accused of killing." She dropped her voice. "The woman he's probably sleeping with."

As Toni was thinking of rounding up the other two angels and heading out, Buddy, the security surveillance guy, came in carrying a black case. With him was a uniformed security guard. As they walked by, she heard him say, "Sometimes they need a little adjusting. The cameras can be temperamental."

He glanced up at that moment and caught Toni's gaze on him. He did that mental run-through where she could see him working out where he'd seen her before then he hit on it. "Toni. Hi." He gave her a thumbs-up. "Everything's under control." And kept walking.

"Who was that?" Tiffany asked. "And how do you know him?"

"I don't. It's a long story."

They'd promised Dwayne a ride home since his car was in the shop, but Dwayne was taking his sweet time. A female fan, a woman in her forties who could lighten up on the eyeliner, seemed to be halting his progress. He drank in her praise the way an alcoholic sucks back booze. She supposed in a way his need for attention was an addiction. She only hoped Tiffany didn't notice what was going on.

She heard the woman ask if he were related to Neil Diamond. She was standing so close to Dwayne that she was going to have his belt buckle imprinted on her navel.

Her ex laughed, that rich laugh of his. "We're distant cousins, but I'd never ride on another man's coattails."

"And I'm cousins with the Queen of England," Linda said softly so only Toni could hear.

Dwayne said, "Thank you, darlin'. I appreciate that. But I'm here with my family." She noticed his sudden passion for his family didn't stop him taking the folded piece of paper the woman slipped him, however.

THE NEXT MORNING, she left the other two sleeping while she went down to the hotel gym for a workout. After all the big meals she'd been eating, she should stay here all day. After grunting and sweating off maybe one pasta dinner, she huffed her way to the health bar and bought three smoothies containing kelp and spinach and some kind of magic energy-boosting compound.

"I brought breakfast," she said when she returned to the room.

Her mother eyed her. "Nothing green could ever be called breakfast, honey."

Her much more health-conscious daughter opened one eye from her bed on the pull-out couch. "Thanks, Mom."

Since she wasn't nearly as health conscious as she wished, she poured herself a cup of coffee from the pot Linda had made in the room.

"A package arrived for you," Linda said, gesturing to a corner. She could be forgiven for not noticing one cardboard shipping box in the midst of the clothes and paraphernalia of three women sharing a room.

"Fantastic." She'd had one of her team pack and ship Loretta Forstman's makeup order so it would arrive as quickly as possible. "I'm going to take it over to her. Tiff? You've got your essay to work on, right?"

"Yes, Mother." In spite of the chaos of their lives, Tiffany was managing to keep up her schoolwork through the wonders of email.

Toni showered, applied her makeup, and dressed in jeans, dress boots and a white shirt. She was ready to kick some butt.

Toni rang Loretta Forstman from the lobby. She hadn't called ahead because she didn't want to be fobbed off with excuses. "Loretta, it's Toni Diamond. I've got your product," she said in her most enthusiastic tones. "I had them put a rush on it because I wanted you to have something special during this difficult time."

"Oh, that's great. Thanks, um—"

Toni could hear a brush-off coming a mile away. She said, "I'm in the lobby. I wanted to bring your product to you myself."

"Okay. Come on up."

Toni knew two things. One: that woman did not want her coming up to her apartment. And two: she could not resist the lure of a bag of brand new cosmetics. Toni had guessed right. Loretta Forstman was a woman after her own heart.

Except for the part where she might be a murderer.

After watching Goldie perform at the club last night, she had to agree with her mother's assessment. It was hard to picture Forstman's girlfriend as a killer.

But Loretta? If she knew her husband was planning to trade her in on a newer model, and that he was about to go bankrupt? Yeah. She could picture it.

She rode the magic elevator to the top, thinking that Loretta could easily have come home, changed clothes and then gone back downstairs again and called her husband from the lobby. Maybe Luke was right and she'd reminded him of their earlier days when they'd frolicked in his office. Who knew?

But somehow she'd been able to get there, kill him and then climb back in the secret elevator and continue on home to her personal trainer and her life insurance money.

But how to prove it?

When she got to the top of the elevator, Loretta was waiting for her. She was standing outside her apartment with the door all but closed. She wore a long sweater so thin it looked like gossamer and must have cost the earth. Tight jeans. Her feet were bare, the nails painted blood red.

"I'd invite you in, but the place is a mess."

"That's all right. I only came to bring you your products," Toni said. "Everything's labeled and I've included the new catalog for easy reordering. Also, my card's in there. You need anything, or you have questions about how to apply it, you call me anytime."

"Thanks, Toni." She looked as excited as a kid on

Christmas morning. "There's just something about brand new makeup that makes me feel like a new woman."

"I know!" Loretta might be a murderer but she shared Toni's enthusiasm for cosmetics and their benefits for a woman's self-esteem as well as her looks.

"Thanks."

Before Loretta could retreat back into her apartment, Toni pulled her in for a hug. "Good luck," she said.

Then she pulled away and turned to call the elevator.

As she got in she realized that she'd got more information from Loretta than she'd bargained on.

The woman's gossamer sweater had been on inside out, like she'd thrown it on in a hurry.

And when she'd pulled her in for a hug, Toni had caught the unmistakable fragrance of Stetson cologne.

When she hit the lobby, Toni wasn't sure what to do. She'd almost yelled Dwayne's name since she knew he was in Loretta's apartment, probably in her bed, at that very moment.

But she didn't. She needed to be smart about this.

There was no way they were partners in Grant Forstman's killing. Dwayne would never take the rap for somebody else. If the cops had picked him up and he knew Loretta had killed her husband, he'd have sung like Pavarotti.

The tape. She needed to see that surveillance tape again.

She'd been so certain the woman in it was Goldie that she hadn't studied it as closely as she should have.

What about the hands? She'd been trying so hard to see a face that she hadn't really studied the hands. As dumb as Goldie was, Toni doubted she'd have worn the big honking diamond if she was planning to kill her lover. But hands

179

could tell a lot about a person's identity. She'd been stupid not to pay more attention.

She only hoped that Buddy was on duty again in the surveillance department. She really didn't want to have to pull out her fake business card and drag out the whole PI routine again.

She thought the chances of bumping into Myrna or Milo were slim, but she kept her eyes open anyway.

As she skulked her way down the corridor to where the surveillance room was, she thought she felt—she wasn't quite sure—a change in the atmosphere. If she had an internal barometer, it was telling her that a storm was approaching.

She picked up the pace, feeling a sense of urgency. But when she rounded the corner to where the room was, she stopped in her tracks.

"Oh, no," she moaned, deep in her throat.

Cops. There were cops swarming like hornets trying to build a nest. In and out of Buddy's office. She crept closer and peeked through the hornet sea and felt as though a million hornets stung her at once.

The body hadn't been moved yet.

The pudgy guy who'd watched surveillance footage with her as though it were a date at the movies was sprawled, his glasses crooked on his face and a stunned expression twisting his mouth.

He was still in the office chair on rolling wheels, slumped as though he was sleeping on the job.

Blood stained his checked shirt.

No, no, NO! She wanted to rewind time the way he'd rewound those tapes, to a time before she'd come in here. Before she'd put that poor man at risk.

Luke was right. She had no business meddling. Now she'd gotten a man killed. She stumbled backward, away from the throng before anyone noticed her. Coming from the other direction was a stretcher and some men in plain clothes.

A young woman in a security uniform sobbed. She was sitting on the floor in the corridor, a hundred feet from the chaos. Her back was against the wall and she had her knees pulled up so she could rest her head on them. A sitting fetal position.

Toni walked up and sat down beside her. Silently, she passed her a tissue.

"Thanks," the woman said, sniffling, then blowing her nose.

Toni passed over the whole pack of tissues. "Did you find him?" Amazingly her voice worked and she sounded normal. Her words echoed in her head as though someone else were speaking them.

The young woman couldn't be more than twenty-five. She had red hair and when she looked up Toni could see that the crying was making her fair complexion blotch. She nodded.

"What time was that?"

"About a...a half hour ago." She pushed both hands up and scrubbed at her wet cheeks. Her hands trembled.

Probably a little longer, Toni guessed. Trauma, as she'd discovered herself, could mess with your sense of time.

"Was he exactly as you found him?"

The girl shuddered. "God, yes. I didn't touch him."

"Why did you go to that room?"

"What?" She sniffed. "Oh, sorry. One of the cameras wasn't working in the casino." Fresh tears fell as she said, "Buddy always fixes them."

She rubbed the girl's arm as she'd do if one of Tiffany's friends came to her with a problem. "Could you see whether anything was missing? Or damaged?"

"No. I saw—him and I freaked. I called 9-1-1. Well, I screamed a little first."

"I'd have screamed too. You didn't see anyone walking away? Anything suspicious?"

The girl looked at her with big, tear-drenched eyes. "You mean, like the murderer? Oh, my God. No."

She didn't know what else to ask. In her gut, Toni already knew what was missing or destroyed. She only hoped Luke had convinced the local cops to get to the footage first.

She contemplated asking to see the detective in charge, but when she considered the matter, she didn't see the point. Besides, she was feeling a little woozy.

She thanked the girl who said, "Can I go now?"

Toni blinked at her. "Don't you need to give the police your statement?"

The girl gaped. "I thought you were the police."

CHAPTER 18

You can avoid reality, but you cannot avoid the consequences of avoiding reality.

— AYN RAND

Toni made her way out onto the hot, crowded sidewalk. She still felt dizzy. To her knowledge, she had never caused anyone's death before but she was pretty sure that if it hadn't been for her, Buddy would still be cracking his knuckles.

She slipped into a fast food place. Ordered an iced tea and sat in a scooped plastic seat clearly designed for the butt of a child and tried to focus. She found her hands were shaking, so she had to hold on to the huge plastic cup with two hands. She was grateful for the straw.

By the time she got to the end of her drink, she felt a little calmer. She suspected that the sight of poor Buddy would haunt her forever, but she couldn't help the dead man by sitting here cowering. All she could do for him now was to get him justice.

She made two phone calls. First, she called Dwayne.

"Darlin'," he said, all warm and sexy. "I was just thinking about you."

From the comforts of another woman's bed. "Dwayne, I need to see you. It's important."

"Well, sure, honey. How about later, you and me—"

"Not later, Dwayne. Now. I'm in—" She named the fast food place. "Come over here. I'll wait."

"Well, sweet pea, I'm in the middle of a business meeting, right now, but—"

"Cut the bull, Dwayne." She'd never used that tone with him before. "Get your butt over here. Now."

And she hung up before he could splutter anything else at her.

The second call was to Luke.

"Marciano."

"Have you heard?"

"Heard what?"

She dropped her head into her hand, fighting the weakness that threatened. "The guy in the security room? He's dead. And he did not die of old age." She dragged in a shaky breath. "Tell me the cops got that footage, Luke."

In the silence she heard something she thought might be computer keys tapping. "Luke?"

"Who did you tell?"

"What?"

His voice sharpened. "Who did you tell about the guy and the footage?"

"You."

"Anyone else? Come on, Toni. Who knew he was holding footage for the cops?"

"No one. I told my mother. No one else."

"You told Linda Plotnik? Might as well have stood on the strip with a megaphone."

His irritation told her everything she needed to know. She closed her eyes. "They didn't get the tape, did they?"

"I don't know. But I doubt they could have moved that fast. They'd need a warrant."

A scrub-your-mouth-out-with-soap word escaped her lips.

"Toni, I want you and Tiffany and your mom on the next plane out of there. I am serious. Whoever killed that guy knows you saw the footage. You are the only person who can implicate her in the murder. I want you out of there, now!"

Luke rarely ordered her around in that way and she knew it was fear making him act like a bully. But she didn't like being bullied. Besides, she'd unwittingly caused a man's death. She couldn't waltz away as though nothing had happened.

"I'll think about it," she said, knowing she wasn't going anywhere until she had nailed the killer. But she was seriously going to put her mother and daughter on the next plane.

"Toni!"

"What!"

"It wasn't your fault."

∾

Dwayne walked in a few minutes later as though there were nowhere else in the world he'd rather be. As though it were his idea they meet here. He shot her his million-watt smile. "Hey, darlin'."

"Don't darlin' me. Sit down."

"Whoa there. Somebody's grumpy." He leaned in to kiss her cheek. His shirt was buttoned properly, his hair was neat. Nothing at all apart from a certain heaviness around his eyes could give Dwayne away that he'd walked straight over from another woman's bed.

Except that they'd mixed fragrances as well as body fluids. His Stetson was mixed with Loretta's perfume.

"I'm going to get a burger and a soda while I'm here. You want anything?"

The thought of food made her ill. "No."

He nodded. Pulled out his wallet and when it opened, she was surprised moths didn't fly out. "Ah, I'm a little short. Could you—"

She slapped a twenty on the plastic table.

While he was getting food, she texted her mom. "Can you book flights home for you and Tiff? ASAP. Will explain later."

Her mom would have a million questions, but Toni deeply believed that her mother would not mess around where her granddaughter was concerned. If Toni said, "Get Tiff out of here," Linda was going to do it.

Dwayne ambled back with a plastic tray containing a hamburger, fries and a giant sized soda. There was no sign of her change.

He bit into the burger, tearing it with strong teeth.

She watched him for a moment. "You worked up quite an appetite."

He shot her a glance from his big blues, but for once had the sense not to answer her. He must have heard her at Loretta's door and if not, Grant's widow would certainly have told him of her visit.

He offered her a fry.

She shook her head. "This business venture that you wanted me to invest in. How's that going?"

He swallowed too fast. Coughed and sucked soda noisily through his straw. "Dangit, woman. What do you want to go asking questions like that when I'm eating?" He coughed again. "There's been a tiny hiccup. But things'll get back on track. Couple of days."

"What is this business venture, exactly?"

He glanced up, half hopeful, half wary. "Why, you interested?"

"Maybe."

Dwayne Diamond might be stupid, but even he wasn't that stupid. He sat back and sucked down a little more cola. "I'm not sure it's right for you. I see you as more of a conservative investor. This is a little risky."

"Indulge me."

He shook his head.

She reached out and grabbed his wrist. "Let me tell you what I think. I think you got conned."

"Conned? What do you take me for?"

Oh, the temptation! But she bit her tongue and resisted answering him. "Those poker chips from the Wentworth? The ones you gave your daughter to go play with?"

She had his attention now. "What about them?"

"They were stolen."

"Now, honey, that's not exactly true."

"Stolen. You know how I know? My mother got caught with them."

He didn't go pale or look startled. He had the natural-born liar's ability to look as innocent as the day he was born. "That's impossible."

"Where did you get ten thousand dollars' worth of casino chips, Dwayne? You can't even pay for a hamburger."

She saw the moment he decided to quit stonewalling her. His shoulders slumped a little and he gave her the heart-melting look of a naughty little boy. "A guy came to me. He's perfected a way to make casino chips. They are so perfect, no one can tell the difference. I paid him a thousand dollars in cash and he gave me ten thousand dollars in chips. He told me to go get a real one and compare them. And he was right. The chips were perfect. He even took me in to play and the dealer didn't blink."

"The dealer?"

"At the Wentworth."

"Did you play at several tables or only one?"

"One. We didn't want to draw attention to ourselves. But I'm telling you, they were good. So he says, if I can get fifty thou, he'll get me half a million in chips. I mean, come on. Half a million dollars. That's the kind of investment I like."

"It's not an investment. It's a crime. Counterfeiting chips is like counterfeiting money. It's against the law."

"The law," he scoffed. "This is Vegas. There is so much money here it's crazy, and don't tell me half of it's not dirty."

"So you came up with fifty grand?"

"No." He shifted on the hard plastic chair. "Thirty."

"Right. The money from Grant Forstman's safe."

He picked up a fry, dipped it in ketchup and then dropped it. "Yeah."

"So, you got, what? Three hundred thousand worth of chips?"

His scowl reminded her of a toddler hearing the word No. "Not exactly. There's been a delay. Some of the equipment broke down."

"You know what I think, Dwayne? I think you got scammed. I think whoever your buddy is was part of an inside job. They stole chips, took you to a dealer who was in on the scam so it seemed like they were legitimate." She wrinkled her nose. "There is no equipment. No one can replicate those chips. Your thirty grand—by which I mean Grant Forstman's thirty grand—is long gone."

"I'm sure you're wrong, honey. I know this guy."

And she knew Dwayne. "Why did you leave the chips in a bowl in your drawer? Why didn't you cash them in right away?"

He shook his head. "They made me promise to wait two months. Something about chip inventory. I didn't completely get it."

"And yet you gave your daughter these chips."

He shrugged. "I figured playing one or two wouldn't mess up their inventory." He tried a grin on her. "And what's the point of having money if you can't spend it on your family?"

"But it wasn't money. It was stolen property."

"No. You'll see—"

"I tell you what else. You'll never see those chips. There are no chips. That thirty thousand is gone, my friend."

He started to bluster but she had a feeling he knew she was right.

"Tell me again how you got into Grant Forstman's safe?"

"I told you. He left his wallet—"

She cut him off. "The truth this time."

He shifted on the chair, looking around the restaurant as though somebody might rescue him. No one did.

She leaned closer. "Do you want me to get you off this murder charge?"

"That money's got nothing to do—"

"I think it does." In fact, things were starting to fall into place. Finally. "Who gave you the combination?"

He licked his lips. "Loretta."

Exactly as she'd thought. "And she gave you the combination to her husband's safe and told you to help yourself to his money out of the goodness of her heart?"

"No. She wanted me to get her something out of the safe, too."

"What?"

"Toni, that's private. I can't tell you—"

"What did you get out of the safe for Loretta?"

"Forstman's life insurance policy."

Bingo.

"Did she tell you why she wanted it?"

"She was afraid he might redeem it for the cash value. She thought it would be safer if she kept it."

She felt the blood drumming in her head. She leaned closer.

"You stole money from the murder victim, lost it all in a scam, and you were having an affair with the dead man's wife. They should put you away and throw away the key."

"But I didn't kill him."

"Not for murder, Dwayne, for stupidity."

CHAPTER 19

Smells are surer than sounds and sights to make heartstrings crack.

— RUDYARD KIPLING

Dwayne left soon after and she took a few minutes to put together pieces of a puzzle that wasn't fitting perfectly. It was like one of those puzzles that contain five hundred pieces of sky, but the last chunk of blue wasn't fitting the pattern.

She walked back to collect her car and on her way called her mom.

"What's up?" Linda asked immediately. "Why are you trying to get rid of me and Tiff?"

"Is she there?"

"No. If she was here I'd speak in code."

Linda's idea of code wouldn't fool a toddler. She did things like spell out words instead of saying them.

"Tiffany needs to get back to school," she said. It wasn't a lie. It was the truth. One of the reasons she wanted her daughter and her mother gone. Not the primary one, but one of them.

Linda sensed she was holding out. There was a slight pause and then her mom said, "Right. Plus, you're trying to protect her."

She was, but how did her mom know?

Then Linda finished her thought. "From seeing what a bonehead Dwayne is."

She thought back to the way her daughter had seen her father take the phone number of that woman after the show and the fact that she'd been sleeping over at the hotel. "I think she is figuring it out, but it's hard for her to have to witness his antics firsthand."

"Sure. I get that. But why aren't you coming back with us?"

She needed to get Linda and Tiff out of town before either of them heard about that second murder. "Because I promised Tiff I'd do my best to keep her father from going to jail for murder." She paused. "Plus, I have to keep an eye on him since I put up my house as collateral for his bail."

"I don't know, Toni. I don't like leaving you here. It doesn't seem right."

"Please. I want Tiffany back at school and seeing her friends again. Frankly, I want her far away from Dwayne, too."

"Ain't that the truth?" Linda agreed. "Tiff's in the shower. I'm just ordering some more product for the boys—"

"More product? Their dressing room won't be big enough," she said with utter admiration at her mother's sales abilities.

Linda giggled. "I know. But they had no idea of proper skincare. I think they're going to be a lot happier now. And, of course, the way they go through makeup, they are going to be great customers for life."

Even the grimness of Buddy's murder couldn't stop her from feeling happy for her mom or from congratulating her.

"So, I'll pack up, you come and get us, and we can go to Brent's house and get Tiffany's stuff, plus I can drop off the product for the boys."

"Sounds good."

"And how about you? Did Loretta Forstman like her product?"

Toni could still smell the mingled scents of Loretta and Dwayne. "I think she liked my ex-husband a whole lot better."

"Oh, mercy, she was not."

"Oh, mercy, she was so."

Her mother's voice changed and the volume went up. "Hi, Tiffany. I'm on the phone with your mom." Toni heard mumbling coming from the phone and then Linda was back, her voice dropped back to almost a whisper. Guaranteed to grab Tiffany's interest. "And don't worry about that other thing. One of these days, DDD will get what's coming to him."

Before her mother could say another word, Toni said, "Okay, I'm on my way."

She retrieved the car and drove back to the hotel. When she got there, Linda was still packing. Tiffany was staring at the TV, which she'd flipped to one of the music video stations. She scowled at her mother. "How come I have to go home?"

The fact that her daughter was complaining that she had to go home and not arguing that she shouldn't be forced to told Toni that her daughter was really happy to be heading back home. But, naturally, she had to put on the front. It was expected.

So, Toni played her role as best she could. She put a hand on her hip, and said, "Because you've already missed too much school and I am putting my foot down. Your dad agrees with me." In fact, when she'd told him at the fast food place that she was taking Tiffany home he'd looked pretty relieved. He was clearly realizing that having a teenaged daughter in town was putting a crimp in his sex life.

"Fine." She rose and slapped off the TV. "Is he going to be home?"

"I don't think so. He was headed back to the Double Nugget last I heard. He wanted to rehearse a new song."

"But I'll get to say goodbye to him, right?"

"Yes. Sure. He's going to come to the airport to say good-bye." Even if she had to haul him out of Loretta's bed and drag him there personally.

"I have to say good-bye to Brent, too. He's at work still."

"You can write him a note."

"Really, Mother? A note?"

"Trust me, it's more polite than email. Brent understands you have to get back to school. Everyone does."

She dug out the notebook she carried everywhere. She flipped through, looking for a blank page to rip out and give to Tiff.

All her recent ideas were in there, a few lists of things she needed to accomplish as soon as she was back home, the notes she'd made about Grant Forstman's murder, some jotted assignments for Tiffany.

The book fell open to the notes she'd jotted down when she'd last been able to have a conference call with her top team members. That had been the very day Dwayne Diamond had called her from out of a clear blue sky looking for money.

They'd both got more than they'd bargained for.

She wished all she had to worry about was making up some fun cards to improve morale. Instead she was trying to prove her ex-husband wasn't a murderer while the real murderer had struck again.

She looked at the slogans.

"When I put on enough makeup, I feel like I'm someone else."

She felt as though pins were pricking every inch of her skin as she stared at those words.

"Mom? Mom!" Tiffany stood with her hand out. "Paper?"

Her brain was turning faster than one of those slot machines Linda was so fond of, patterns forming, reforming, so she couldn't keep anything straight.

Finally, the whirring stopped and as though she had a readout in front of her, that might or might not pay out, she knew what she had to do.

"Honey, I just remembered, I've got to pick something up. Why don't you help Grandma finish her packing? I'll pick you up a nice note card that says thank you on it. A torn piece of notepaper isn't the Diamond way."

Her daughter looked at her as though she was crazy, but that was how her daughter looked at her most of the time so Toni wasn't worried. "Whatever."

She went back and flipped the TV back on. She didn't even notice that Toni palmed Brent's house key, the one he'd lent her so she could come and go from his house.

What she needed to do now, she needed to do alone.

Please let me be wrong about this, Toni said to herself as she parked in front of Brent's house. If anyone asked, she was here to pack up Tiffany's belongings. She also had a little side business that she was keeping to herself.

She could be in and out in thirty minutes, before Brent or Dwayne returned home. Then she'd scoop up her mother and daughter and have them at the airport in plenty of time for their evening flight.

She might even be on that flight with them. Everything depended on whether her hunch was correct.

Toni rang the bell in case anyone was home, but the echo of the bell died away and no one came to the door. She used the key to let herself in and called out, "Anybody home?"

Nothing but silence greeted her.

She stepped in, closed the door behind her. She stood for a moment and listened. Nothing. She could smell the faintest hint of Lady Bianca face cream.

She walked through the empty rooms. At Dwayne's bedroom she hesitated, then knocked on the closed door. No answer. She opened it and confirmed that he was out. His guitar was gone too, so presumably he was at the casino working on his act. Or crooning love songs to some woman, somewhere, who ought to know better.

She peeked next into the guest room where Tiff had been staying. Fortunately, most of Tiff's stuff was at the hotel. What little was left would take her about ten minutes to pack.

She took a deep breath. The best way to get through a

difficult task, she always told her new recruits, was to put a big smile on your face and power through it. That might work with cold calling and friendly fishing, but for what she was about to do, she thought she could forgo the big smile.

She pulled her cell phone out of her bag, clicked to camera mode. Headed to Brent's bedroom. There was a part of her that felt truly bad invading Brent's privacy this way, but she needed to know the truth.

Her footsteps were silent on the thick rug. She got to Brent's door. Knocked.

Nothing.

She opened the door and called his name softly, but there was no answer. She could sense the emptiness in the room. With a quick pep talk to herself, she flipped on his bedroom light and stepped inside.

Her mother had told her that his bedroom made the living room appear tame, but she'd assumed Linda was exaggerating.

She hadn't been.

Her first thought was of an ice palace. Everything was white and glittered. Huge mirrors, a white shag rug, a king-sized bed with a white satin bedspread, a silver headboard and so many sequined pillows they made her eyes hurt.

The walls were pure white, the molding silver. Enormous black and white photographs dominated the white walls. A showgirl posing in the sixties, she'd guess from the clothing worn by the patrons.

When she opened the double doors, lights immediately illuminated the largest walk-in closet she had ever seen. A short rack on the left held the somewhat meager and entirely dull wardrobe of Brent Hodgkin, CPA.

Every other inch of space was devoted to Sunny. Gowns, headdresses, an entire mirrored dresser for wigs. Rack upon rack of shoes.

She smelled powder and the faint scent of perfume, almost like an echo from an earlier time.

The gowns were luscious, glittering things, most of them carefully stored in individual garment bags.

Her heart was pounding, and she felt a shiver of claustrophobia as she walked deeper into the closet.

Black. She only wanted to look at the black outfits.

His system wasn't to put like colors together, but to assemble gowns that would be worn for similar purposes.

Over-the-top show gowns together. Evening gowns together. Street clothes, if any of it could be classified as street clothes, together.

She flipped rapidly through day wear, increasingly hopeful that she was wrong.

She began searching through evening wear, flipping rapidly through each outfit. The odd garment bag wasn't transparent so, after she'd checked every outfit she could see, she started on the ones that needed to be unzipped to display their contents.

She found what she was looking for in the third bag. Carefully, she unzipped the fastening and was greeted by black silk. She drew the padded hanger off the rack and carried the bag out to the bedroom. She laid the bag on the bed and rapidly unzipped it all the way.

"No," she moaned when she'd revealed a silk jacket and pants that she recognized. "Oh, no." Somewhere in that rack of wigs in the cupboard would be the one that so resembled Loretta and Goldie's hairstyle. He'd been impersonating women for years. He'd done a superb job for the security camera.

Her hand was trembling as she raised her cell phone.

"I should have burned that, of course," Brent's voice said, just behind her.

With a tiny squeak of surprise mingled with panic, she turned to find Brent Hodgkin standing just inside the door to his bedroom, the one she'd so foolishly left wide open.

She fumbled with the phone.

He wore a brown suit with a tie the color of swamp mud paired with a cream shirt. His hair was neatly brushed, his brown loafers shone with recent polish. She could only imagine he kept the gun he was pointing at her in as tip-top condition.

"But the outfit was Mother's. I could not bring myself to destroy it. She wore it for him, you know. That's why I put it on that night. Sentiment, I suppose."

"The night you killed him, you mean."

Toni was fairly certain that the gun had killed not only Grant Forstman but also Buddy Olafson, the security guy who'd been in charge of video surveillance. Brent wouldn't hesitate to kill her.

If she could drag this out, maybe she had a chance.

In spite of the fact that he was a cold-blooded murderer, she couldn't help a stab of pity for Brent. "Grant Forstman was your father, wasn't he?"

He nodded. "Don't you think one bad thought about my mother. She wasn't a loose woman. He was going to marry her. They were engaged. But he met somebody else and broke her heart." His voice trembled ever so slightly. "She loved him."

"Did he know about you?"

His lips compressed. "He gave her some money. Paid her off. But he refused to see her or me." He shook his head. "My mother died of a broken heart, Toni. And I swore I'd avenge her death."

"How did you find out about the secret elevator?"

He made a derisive sound. "Please. Goldie couldn't keep a secret if her life depended on it. She was so full of herself, becoming the next Mrs. Forstman, that she told me everything. It was so easy. All I had to do was get rid of the bodyguards and pretend to be her."

"The food poisoning?"

"They eat like pigs. Easy enough to slip something in their food."

"But only one of them got sick."

"Didn't matter. Forstman was so paranoid of getting sick that he stayed clear of Milo that whole day."

She nodded, remembering what Dwayne had told her. "He sent him home early. But why did you set Dwayne up to take the rap?"

"Look, Toni, no offense to your ex-husband, but Dwayne set himself up. He stole from Forstman, was banging his wife, I figured I did him a favor. He was better off in jail than getting taken out by Forstman's thugs. They'd have done it, too."

"Taken out? You mean like—"

"Rubbed out, digging holes in the desert, erased, disappeared—"

"Okay, murdered. I get it."

"Forstman wasn't a good guy to tangle with and Dwayne

was like a bug crawling under his raised boot. He was asking for trouble."

It was twisted logic but she didn't imagine most killers used straight logic or they would never kill in the first place. "So, you were doing Dwayne a favor?"

He shrugged. "We were doing each other a favor. Your ex was in the wrong place at the wrong time, and since Dwayne didn't kill Forstman, I figured there was a good chance he'd get off. Meanwhile, he was so convenient, on the scene, looking guiltier than sin. What was the incentive for the cops to search deeper?" He scowled. "Everything was going fine. Then you came along."

"My daughter came along first." And for that, if nothing else, she would never forgive Brent. He'd committed murder while her daughter was staying in his home. Worse, he'd set up his house guest's father for the crime.

He seemed to feel mildly ashamed of himself. "Yeah. That timing was unfortunate. She's a great kid." He shrugged. "But she's tough. She'll be fine. And Linda will do a great job looking after her."

Right, because he was planning to kill Toni, of course.

She needed to think, and she needed to think fast. This guy had killed not only once, he'd killed twice, the second time an innocent man who happened to be in the way. She knew he wouldn't hesitate to kill her.

Unless she could stop him.

Linda was a great mom and a great grandma, he was right. But Toni wasn't ready to let her take over Tiff's upbringing so some pathetic guy with an overdeveloped mommy complex could get away with murder.

"How did you get Grant Forstman to let you up?"

In a second, she watched Brent's face soften and transform ever so slightly. He pushed out his lips, cocked a hip. "Honey? It's me, and I've got a little itch I need my big boy to scratch." The man was an incredible mimic. If she'd had her eyes closed she'd have believed Goldie was in the room.

"She does not really say things like that."

"Oh, she does." He seemed as nauseated as she was. "I'd been listening in on her calls to him."

"And he said, 'Come on up?'"

He pursed his lips, went back to being Brent. "I will not offend my mother's memory by repeating his exact words, but yes. He pushed the button to let Goldie up to his office."

"I bet he was surprised to see you."

"I made very sure he understood exactly who I was and why I was there."

"And then you killed him."

"I did it for Mother."

"And what about Buddy? He never hurt you. He didn't deserve to die."

He shook his head, looking peevish. "Buddy's all on you. I didn't have any problem with you trying to get Dwayne off the hook. Hey, he's a friend of mine."

She almost snorted her disbelief but held herself back. That gun had not wavered from pointing in the general direction of her chest. She didn't want to irritate Brent enough that he'd pull the trigger.

"If you wanted to make Loretta look bad, I had no problem with that. She was a slut, anyway. I didn't even think to get rid of the footage from the security cameras. That was sloppy of me. When Buddy spoke to you that night in the club, I realized how stupid I'd been. And I took care of it."

He explained these things to her as though they were perfectly reasonable. Like one of those math equations he'd helped Tiffany with. Step one leads inevitably to step two, and if this happens then that happens.

But Toni did not fit the pattern. "There is no way you can kill me and get away with it. You might as well give yourself up to the police. Honestly, Brent. Everybody will understand that you did what you thought was right for your mother." And she glossed over about what everybody would think about him murdering an innocent man in cold blood whose only crime was possessing film that implicated Brent. "I already have the names of some good lawyers from when Dwayne was charged. But if you kill me, well, my boyfriend's a cop. They won't rest until you are put away for life." She paused for dramatic effect. "Or worse."

He smiled. As though she were one of his less bright clients and she was trying to tell him why her poodle sitter was a tax-deductible expense.

"Don't worry. I'll fix it all up nice and neat and tidy."

Oh, this she really had to hear. "How?"

"Pick up your cell phone and call Dwayne."

"Dwayne? Why would I call him?"

"Because he needs to come home. And when he does, you're going to argue and tell him exactly why you know he murdered Grant Forstman. He'll go psycho and kill you. Then, in remorse, he'll kill himself." He glanced at the firearm in his hand. "With this gun, of course."

A shiver of pure dread slithered down her spine. Not that Brent would get away with his insane plan, but that by the time he was caught she and Dwayne would already be dead.

"Well, I'm not going to call Dwayne."

He looked for a second as though he was going to shoot her now and figure out the rest later. A spark of pure crazy flashed in his eyes, and she took a step back until she bumped the bed with the back of her knees.

Come on, Toni. She had to think of something.

"Give me your phone."

"Or what?"

"Or I'll shoot you in the leg. I'm a very good shot. I've been practicing for a long time."

She picked up the phone. Clicked a button. She tossed it, harder than necessary and in the direction of his face. All she needed was a moment of inattention, for him to jerk back or have to pick up the phone from the floor.

Brent surprised her yet again. His reflexes were too good. He grabbed the flying phone with his left hand while the gun in his right hand barely wavered.

He found Dwayne's number on her cell, never letting his attention or gun waver. He glanced at her. "I'm sure you know enough about guns to recognize a silencer. If you do anything stupid like try to yell something, you'll be dead before you get the first word out. Do you understand?"

She sent him a glance so sour she hoped it withered his liver. She nodded.

He pushed send.

Don't pick up, she begged.

"Toni, darlin'," she heard her ex-husband say, loud and clear.

Oh, please gush right back, she begged Brent silently. Then Dwayne would know something was up.

But Brent had obviously been listening to her and

Dwayne as closely as he'd listened to Goldie's conversations with Grant Forstman.

"Dwayne," Brent said in a tone that sounded more like her mother than like Toni. "I'm at Brent's house. I need to talk to you. Can you come right over?"

"Why sure, darlin'. What's up?"

Brent rolled his gaze. "Somebody dropped off some money. Said it's for you."

He whooped. She could hear him as clearly as though he'd been in the same room. "Didn't I tell you my ship was comin' in? I got my car back, too. I'm on my way. Don't move. I'll be right there. And I am taking you and Tiff and Linda for the biggest steak dinner you ever saw."

As Brent ended the call, he shook his head. "That was almost too easy."

"Please, Brent," she said. "Please don't do this." She thought maybe she could manage a few tears, and by thinking about Tiffany losing both her parents, managed easily. If Brent considered she was weak and frightened he might let his guard waver.

Which would be a great plan if she wasn't frightened and, compared to a wiry guy with great reflexes and a loaded gun, she did feel pretty weak.

However, she had Tiffany to think of and no female-impersonating, mommy-obsessed murderer was going to get rid of her. Not without the fight of her life.

Everybody has weaknesses. She already knew his. His obsessive love for his mother. And hatred for his father.

While they waited, she got him talking about his mother. As she'd suspected, she was the showgirl in the photographs dominating this room. Brent could talk all day, but he wasn't going to let his guard down. Not for a second.

In all too short a time, she heard loud country music, which suggested that Dwayne had the top down on his convertible and was outside.

Brent heard it too.

He said, "You're not going to do anything stupid and you know why?"

She shook her head, still trying to look weak and frightened.

"Because if you screw this up, I will call Tiffany and tell her you're in trouble and you need her."

She felt the rage of a mother tiger rise within her, fought to keep it from showing. "No. Please. I'll do anything you say."

He smiled briefly. Nodded. "You keep your mouth shut and do everything I say."

The front door banged open and Dwayne called out, "Hey, Toni. I'm home. Where's my gorgeous wife?"

"Ex-wife," Brent snapped in exactly the tone Toni used. Wow, he was good. "I'm down here in Brent's room."

"What are you doing in Brent's room?" Dwayne asked. She could hear him getting closer.

"I've got a surprise for you."

"And I've got a surprise for you," Toni said.

She'd grabbed the garment bag and dragged the zipper up into the black silk, mangling it horribly.

She held the outfit in front of her hoping that Brent wouldn't put a bullet through one of his precious mother's outfits.

A cry of rage came from the man holding the gun on her. "Stop that," he spat.

"Honey?" Dwayne ambled into the open doorway, a big smile on his face and his guitar in his hand.

She saw the second Dwayne caught sight of Brent and the gun. That moment she'd made him crazy had given her a split second. It was all she was going to get.

With all the strength of a mother tiger with a cub to protect, she launched herself at Brent, the gown, still in its protective cover, held in front of her like a shield.

"What the?" Dwayne yelled.

She smashed into Brent, wrapping the bag around his face and knocking him over. He screamed, staggered, and she hooked a foot behind his calf in a move she'd learned in a women's self-defense class. But he was a lot stronger than she was and if she had the strength of a mother tiger, he had the strength of a cornered lion.

The garment bag was slippery in her hands and she was hopping on one heel trying to trip Brent. Dwayne stood staring like the statue of a country and western singer, something you'd see on a Nashville sidewalk.

In desperation she went with a last-ditch move.

She kneed Brent in the balls.

He huffed out a breath as he started to double over. And then she heard a second huff. The muffled sound of a bullet.

Burning pain, like a hot poker stabbing her. Her left side was on fire.

She staggered back to the bed, struggling to breathe.

Brent was like something out of a horror movie, rising, his head caught in the open bag, black silk hanging over his face.

He batted at the encumbrance.

"Dwayne," she yelled. "He's going to kill us."

Her ex finally snapped out of his stupor. The garment bag

fell away from Brent and he righted his crooked glasses, turned toward Dwayne, leveling the gun. In that moment, Dwayne raised the guitar over his head and brought it down on top of Brent's head.

She watched the man who'd killed two people and tried to kill her and Dwayne fall to the ground. Her vision was blurry and she could feel the wetness of blood running down her arm, but she managed to kick the gun out of Brent's nerveless hand.

As she sank to the ground she heard sirens. "Thank goodness," she said and then everything went black.

CHAPTER 20

Selfishness must always be forgiven you know, because there is no hope of a cure.

— JANE AUSTEN

Toni opened her eyes, wondering where she was. Nothing seemed familiar. The smell was awful, like a hospital. She blinked and realized that the place smelled like a hospital because she was in one.

Her arm hurt. Her throat was dry. Her lips felt naked as though there was no lipstick on them.

She must have made a sound, for a figure rose from a chair and came toward her.

She recognized the dark hair and sexy eyes, the cop face. "Luke?" Her voice sounded rusty.

His expression lightened and she saw the relief as he smiled down at her. "How are you feeling?"

"Like I need a day at the spa."

"That's my girl." He leaned over and kissed her.

"Am I in Texas?" She had hazy memories but they were coming back thick and fast.

"No, honey. You're in Vegas."

"But why are you here?"

"I am here on official police business." He picked up a paper cup with a straw in it and passed it to her as though he knew how thirsty she was. She sucked some water thankfully.

"Is Tiffany okay? My mom?"

"They're fine. We're taking turns sitting with you."

She had so many questions but one was paramount. "Brent?"

"He confessed on my cell phone. Remember?"

She nodded then winced. Everything hurt. "I was going to call you and tell you what I'd found." She sucked some more water. "And then I heard him behind me. I hit speed dial. Wasn't sure you were even there."

"Oh, I was there." He ran a hand through his short hair. "I recorded most of it, and got through to LVPD as fast as I could." His mouth twisted. "But not fast enough."

"I thought he'd killed me."

For a second his eyes were bleak with rage and maybe grief, but in the overbright lighting it was hard to be certain, the cop shutters came down so fast. "I thought so, too. Last thing I heard was him ordering you to give him your cell phone so he could lure Dwayne there and kill both of you."

"That was a bad moment."

"For both of us." He took her hand. The one that didn't have tubes coming out of it.

"What happened to Brent?"

"He's in police custody."

"Dwayne? Is he okay?"

In an expressionless voice, he said, "Right about the time the cops arrived, your ex-husband came running out of the house screaming for help. He left you inside wounded and with a psycho killer for company."

"Did he at least take the gun with him?"

Luke shook his head.

Somehow she wasn't surprised.

"Luckily, the cops and the paramedics arrived around the same time. They got to Hodgkin before he regained consciousness and to you before you bled out."

"At least Dwayne knocked him on the head with his guitar."

"To save you or his own skin?"

She did her best to squeeze the hand holding hers, so warm and sure. "I believe I mentioned I have better taste in men now?"

"You sure do." He held the cup so she could sip more water. "After they played Hodgkin the recording I made on my phone, he confessed. Naturally, his lawyer is going for a psych defense."

She suspected Brent was crazy but didn't have the energy to argue with Luke at the moment. She was too glad to see him.

THEY KEPT her in hospital for a couple more days. She'd been incredibly lucky, the doctor told her. The bullet had grazed her side and only cracked a rib. It was the blood loss that was making her feel so weak. She'd always bear a scar, but she was vain enough to be happy that it was in an area where it wouldn't be too noticeable.

Linda and Tiffany refused to fly home, but spent every minute they could with Toni. Thanks to her mother, Toni was the best-groomed patient in the hospital. Thanks to Tiff, she was the best entertained. Her daughter was so much on her best behavior it was almost painful. When she wasn't working on homework, she was thinking up ideas to help Toni grow her business. She'd even taken to wearing color.

"It's unnerving," Toni said to Linda when Tiff was out of the room.

"It's because she almost lost you." Her mom sighed. "Don't worry. She'll soon get over it."

At one point, while Linda was painting Tiffany's nails a real color, and they were going over the unbelievable events one more time, Tiff said, "I can't believe I shared a house with a murderer. *Eew*."

Linda paused in the application of a very pretty soft pink color to her granddaughter's fingernails. "And let that be a reminder to you to always listen to your mother." And then she went on painting nails.

ONCE SHE WAS RELEASED from hospital, Toni still needed to go to the cops and give her statement.

Luke insisted on driving her, and waiting for her, then driving her back to the hotel.

"Thanks," she said.

"For what?"

"Being a man I can count on."

His expression was skeptical. "If you're comparing me with Dwayne, that's not much of a compliment."

She looked him right in the eye. "I wasn't." And she leaned over and kissed him.

They were leaving the next day. Toni hadn't been allowed to so much as pack her own toothbrush. Her daughter and her mother had done everything.

"Now, I want you to have a nap," Linda told Toni, "because we are going out tonight."

"We are? Where?"

"Dwayne wants us to go to the casino. He's got a new song he wrote especially for you."

She shuddered. "I'm not sure I can go back there."

"We kind of promised we'd go," Tiffany said. She threw her arms around Toni, but carefully. "I am so sorry, Mom. I never should have come here without telling you."

She hugged back. Also carefully. "But it turned out to be a good thing. You got to know your father and we helped him out of a very big jam."

"I think he's really sorry, too. That's why he wants us there tonight."

Her mother leaned forward. "And wait until you see the new Sunny." She fanned herself.

Toni looked at her. "He's gorgeous or you're having a hot flash?"

Her mom continued to fan herself. "Actually, both.'"

Luke had flown back that morning to get back to work,

and both Linda and Tiffany had promised him they'd keep an eye on Toni.

Apart from a little weakness and some pain at the wound site, Toni felt pretty good. Her mother and daughter made her stay in bed all afternoon so they could go to the casino that night.

Her mom did her makeup since it hurt too much to lift her arm and they helped her dress.

The lounge didn't look any different than it had before two people had been murdered and one of the cast turned out to be the killer.

A Reserved sign sat on one of the prime tables and the server who showed them to it said, "Dwayne's real excited you're here. He wrote a song specially for you, isn't that sweet?"

Since he'd nearly got her killed and her daughter orphaned, she wasn't sure a song was going to cut it, but she smiled politely and let Tiffany help her into a chair. Not that she needed help, but it was so nice to have her daughter treat her so well she was kind of milking it.

Toni was surprised to see Loretta in the audience. Not only did Grant Forstman's widow come over and say hello and tell her that she'd be ordering more of that amazing face cream real soon, but she sent a round of drinks to the table.

The show was familiar but not. During the Broadway number she realized that Forstman's girlfriend wasn't there. She kind of missed watching her count her steps. "What happened to Goldie?" she asked her mom. She hoped Loretta hadn't fired the girl.

Linda leaned close. "She got a better offer."

"From another casino?" Toni couldn't imagine.

"From another big shot. Guy from Atlanta."

Toni chuckled. "Good for her."

When the familiar theme music came for Sunny and the Three Chers, she stiffened. It was going to be tough to sit through this part of the show and not remember...

And then she forgot all about Brent Hodgkin when the most gorgeous blond Toni had ever seen strode onto the stage. S/he looked slightly familiar and she couldn't figure out where she'd seen the female impersonator before. The Three Chers tottered on behind and as they broke into their first song, she noted that Sunny had the tiniest hint of a Scandinavian accent. And that Loretta was clapping so hard her fake nails were in danger of flying off her fingertips.

"That's Eric," she whispered to her mom. "He's Loretta's personal trainer."

"Training her to do what exactly?"

"Shh. He's a hell of an entertainer. And he's got every single person in the audience, the men and the women, completely in love." From that moment on she let herself relax and enjoy, not the show that had been, but the show that was going on right in front of her.

When the wild applause for the new Sunny and the Three Chers had died down, the MC gave a longer than normal intro for Dwayne.

It was so glowing she suspected money had changed hands.

And then her ex-husband walked into the spotlight. He wore black relieved only with the silver buckle on his belt and the rhinestones on the piping of his dress shirt. Even his cowboy hat was black.

He cozied up to the mic as though it were a lover and said,

"This is the song I wrote for an amazing woman, a lady who will always own a piece of my heart. We've been through a lot together, darlin', and I want you to know how much you mean to me."

He glanced around at the audience, then back to their table. "There are moments that change a man forever. And this song is the true story of one of those moments."

He strummed a little, warming up, he said, "This goes out to Toni and it's called, 'I Saved Your Life Tonight.'"

There was a choking sound at their table. She wasn't sure if it was coming from her, from Linda, or the two of them were performing a gagging duet.

"I Saved Your Life Tonight" was a simple ballad about a man who loved and lost a woman, a woman who was the mother of his child. She came back into his life and he almost lost her again when another man tried to harm her. But, in the nick of time, the singer hero, i.e. Dwayne, rushed to the rescue. The end of the song told the world that even though their time was past, he'd always be her man, "Because I saved your life tonight."

When he finished, she caught a woman at another table dabbing her eyes with a tissue. Linda gulped her margarita down, probably to drown out her own commentary on the song in Tiffany's hearing.

Afterward, Dwayne swaggered up to their table, a big smile on his face.

"Hi, Dad," Tiffany said.

"How's my gorgeous girl?" he asked, giving her a one-armed hug.

"Fine."

"And how are you feeling, Toni?" He reached over and

patted her shoulder. Luckily, not on the side where she'd been shot.

"I'm fine."

He shook his head, playing to the table, and then turned to Tiffany. "I tell you, facing a killer to save your mom was one of the toughest moments of my life. But every man needs to know what he's made of. He needs to know that he can dig deep and when someone he loves is in trouble, he can step up and be a hero."

Did he think she had amnesia? She recalled him standing there with a stunned look on his face while Brent nearly killed her. It was only after Brent tottered to his feet and turned the gun in Dwayne's direction that he'd finally bashed the guy over the head with his guitar. And, according to Luke, he'd then gone screaming out of the house to save his own skin.

He must have assumed her inability to speak was from gratitude. He turned to her. "I'm so happy I was there to save your life."

She thought about how he'd got all of them into this mess, and how he was the one who'd nearly got them killed.

But Tiffany was sitting at the table, and even if Dwayne was a dimwit, he'd given her a daughter to be proud of.

And, maybe he had almost got her killed, but in the end he'd helped her stop Brent.

Tomorrow, she'd be on a plane back home with a daughter who had finally come to know her father, and she'd seen his flaws as well as his charm. She and Tiff were on better terms than they'd been in months.

When she'd opened her eyes in the hospital and seen

Luke at her bedside, the look in his eyes had told her more than he'd ever tell her in words.

Plus, she and her mom had both acquired some terrific new clients.

Dwayne had caused her a lot of suffering in her life, but he'd given her the greatest treasure she could imagine.

"I'm glad you were there, too."

A Note from Nancy

Dear Reader,

Thank you for reading *Ultimate Concealer*. I am so grateful for all the enthusiasm the *Toni Diamond Mysteries* has received.

I hope you'll consider leaving a review and please tell your friends who like cozy mysteries.

Review on Amazon, Goodreads or BookBub.

Don't let the fun end. Let's stay in touch.

Join my newsletter to hear about my new releases and enjoy prizes and bonus content like the Vampire Knitting Club's free prequel, *Tangles and Treasons*, the exciting tale of how the gorgeous Rafe Crosyer was turned into a vampire.

I hope to see you in my private Facebook Group Nancy Warren's Knitwits where the fun continues daily.

Until next time,
Happy Reading,

Nancy

Vampire Knitting Club: Cornwall: Paranormal Cozy Mystery

Boston-bred witch Jennifer Cunningham agrees to run a knitting and yarn shop in a fishing village in Cornwall, England—with characters from the Oxford-set *Vampire Knitting Club* series.

The Vampire Knitting Club: Cornwall - Book 1

Scallops and Sorcerers - Book 2

Village Flower Shop: Paranormal Cozy Mystery

In a picture-perfect Cotswold village, flowers, witches, and murder make quite the bouquet for flower shop owner Peony Bellefleur.

Peony Dreadful - Book 1

Karma Camellia - Book 2

Highway to Hellebore - Book 3

Luck of the Iris - Book 4

Game of Thorns - Book 5

Vampire Book Club: Paranormal Women's Fiction Cozy Mystery

Seattle witch Quinn Callahan's midlife crisis is interrupted when she gets sent to Ballydehag, Ireland, to run an unusual bookshop.

Crossing the Lines - Prequel

The Vampire Book Club - Book 1

Chapter and Curse - Book 2

A Spelling Mistake - Book 3

A Poisonous Review - Book 4

In Want of a Knife - Book 5

Vampire Book Club Boxed Set: Books 1-3

Great Witches Baking Show: Paranormal Culinary Cozy Mystery

Poppy Wilkinson, an American with English roots, joins a reality show to win the crown of Britain's Best Baker—and to get inside Broomewode Hall to uncover the secrets of her past.

The Great Witches Baking Show - Book 1

Baker's Coven - Book 2

A Rolling Scone - Book 3

A Bundt Instrument - Book 4

Blood, Sweat and Tiers - Book 5

Crumbs and Misdemeanors - Book 6

A Cream of Passion - Book 7

Cakes and Pains - Book 8

Whisk and Reward - Book 9

Gingerdead House - A Holiday Whodunnit

The Great Witches Baking Show Boxed Set: Books 1-3

The Great Witches Baking Show Boxed Set: Books 4-6 (includes bonus novella)

The Great Witches Baking Show Boxed Set: Books 7-9

Abigail Dixon: 1920s Cozy Historical Mystery

In 1920s Paris everything is très chic, except murder.

Murder at the Paris Fashion House - Book 1

Death at Darrington Manor - Book 2

The Almost Wives Club: Contemporary Romantic Comedy

An enchanted wedding dress is a matchmaker in this series of romantic comedies where five runaway brides find out who the best men really are.

The Almost Wives Club: Kate - Book 1

Secondhand Bride - Book 2

Bridesmaid for Hire - Book 3

The Wedding Flight - Book 4

If the Dress Fits - Book 5

The Almost Wives Club Boxed Set: Books 1-5

Take a Chance: Contemporary Romance

Meet the Chance family, a cobbled together family of eleven kids who are all grown up and finding their ways in life and love.

Chance Encounter - Prequel

Kiss a Girl in the Rain - Book 1

Iris in Bloom - Book 2

Blueprint for a Kiss - Book 3

Every Rose - Book 4

Love to Go - Book 5

The Sheriff's Sweet Surrender - Book 6

The Daisy Game - Book 7

Take a Chance Boxed Set: Prequel and Books 1-3

For a complete list of books, check out Nancy's website at NancyWarrenAuthor.com

ABOUT THE AUTHOR

Nancy Warren is the USA Today Bestselling author of more than 70 novels. She's originally from Vancouver, Canada, though she tends to wander and has lived in England, Italy and California at various times. Favorite moments include being the answer to a crossword puzzle clue in Canada's National Post newspaper, being featured on the front page of the New York Times when her book Speed Dating launched Harlequin's NASCAR series, and being nominated three times for Romance Writers of America's RITA award. She has an MA in Creative Writing from Bath Spa University. She's an avid hiker, loves chocolate and most of all, loves to hear from readers! The best way to stay in touch is to sign up for Nancy's newsletter at www.nancywarren.net.

To learn more about Nancy and her books
www.nancywarren.net